This enchanting book of mischief and magic
belongs to

....

Mischief & Magic

Enchanting Tales of India

A RETELLING

ILLUSTRATED BY PRIYAL MOTE

Editor Ayushi Thapliyal
Art Editor and Illustrator Priyal Mote

Pre-production Manager Narender Kumar
Jacket Designer Priyal Mote

Managing Editor Chitra Subramanyam
Managing Art Editor Neha Ahuja Chowdhry

Managing Director, India Aparna Sharma

Retold by Ayushi Thapliyal, Priyanka Kharbanda, Chitra Subramanyam

First published in India in 2019 by
Dorling Kindersley Publishing Private Limited,
208, Ansal's Laxmi Deep
Laxmi Nagar District Centre
New Delhi 110092, India

A Penguin Random House Company
10 9 8 7 6 5 4 3 2 1
001–316546–Nov/2019

A CIP catalogue record for this book is available from The British Library.

ISBN: 978-0-2414-2983-9

Printed and bound in India.

A WORLD OF IDEAS:
SEE ALL THERE IS TO KNOW

www.dk.com

Introduction

We have all grown up on stories. Narrated by parents, grandparents, and teachers, these stories have enriched our lives, shaped our thinking, and transported us into a world of fantasy and imagination. Some stories helped us learn important lessons in life and understand the good from the bad, while others helped us become who we are as adults. Well-told stories have the power to bring characters to life and capture the imagination of the young reader.

At the same time, reading together is precious for a parent and child, especially in the early days, as it helps create a lifelong bond and builds an everlasting love for reading. This was something I looked forward to at the end of each day, snuggling up with my son and his favourite book, giggling and laughing as we read together at bedtime.

So, when we sat down to plan this book, our aim was to create something truly special for every child. We wanted to bring together stories from different parts of the country and from many faiths so that every child finds a tale that resonates with him or her.

The stories and folk tales in this book have been drawn from many sources, including the Jataka tales, the Katha Sarit Sagara of the 11th century, the Puranas, the Quran, and the Janamsakhis. With beautiful, original illustrations bringing them to life, this collection of tales is an attempt to retell stories of the past, adapt them to the changing times of today, and engage and entertain the young reader while imparting important life lessons through mischief and magic.

Join us on this enchanting journey.

Aparna Sharma
Managing Director, DK India

Contents

The First Darkness

A folk tale from Central India

When the world was young, the sun would always shine. There was no yesterday, or tomorrow, or even the day after tomorrow, just Today.

Today was never dark which is why no one slept. But, there were moments when the sun's rays were so intense, they would destroy crops, dry up ponds, and even make babies and children cry.

The world was still being made and the Creator had many things to figure out – where the lakes, rivers, seas, and oceans would go or which animals would live in the mountains, by the rivers, or in the plains and forests. More than anything else, the Creator wanted to help the humans and often visited the world below to see how things were.

One day, the Creator heard babies wailing out of exhaustion and hunger, and the people complaining of failing crops. Everyone sounded tired and quite fed up. It was time to visit Earth once again.

The Creator descended on to a field of rice. There were some tired-looking women and men listlessly ploughing the land.

On seeing them, the Creator said, "This field must have taken a while to plough. When did you begin?"

Everyone replied in unison, "We cultivated this field Today".

"Today?" asked the Creator confused. "How is that possible?"

A farmer spoke up, "Today, we tilled this piece of land with the help of buffaloes and bullock carts. Sowed the seeds that you gave us. Flooded it with water. Then Today, we watched the saplings grow. After that we de-weeded the crop saplings, watched them grow again, plucked the fully grown grains, and separated the husk from the rice. And now, Today, we are getting ready for the next harvest."

Taken aback by their response, the Creator took notes and walked a bit further, towards a beautiful and green garden speckled with yellow marigolds, purple chrysanthemums, pink carnations, and white tuberose flowers. Amazed, the Creator asked: "When did you create such an exquisite garden?"

Everyone stopped working in the garden and seemed bemused. One of the gardeners piped up: "We found this piece of land Today, tilled the soil and added cow dung to fertilize the soil. Today, we sowed the flower seeds that you gave us. And then today, we watered the soil and watched as the flower grew." The Creator was flummoxed by the answer, but made notes anyway.

Suddenly, the Creator heard hammering and walked to the wood shop. A carpenter was adding finishing touches to a bench she had made. The Creator asked, "When did you carve this exquisite seat?"

"Today, I spotted a fallen Sal tree, cut it into logs, pruned the splinters, smoothed out the log, and carved the bench," she answered. "And Today, I am polishing the surface."

By now, many people who had followed the Creator, gathered around. In one voice they spoke: "With all due respect, why don't you understand? We've done everything Today!"

The Creator had one last question. "When did I last visit you?"

And the crowd chanted in unison, "Today. You last came Today."

"What am I missing? Why do they think that everything happened today?" The Creator wondered, and finally realized that the people did not know how to measure time.

The Sun was summoned. The Creator said, "You must now rest and set. We will call this Night. Then after half the time has passed, I will call upon you again and you will rise. That will be Day." The Sun was happy with the terms as he was also tired of shining constantly and desperately needed a break.

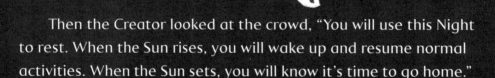

Then the Creator looked at the crowd, "You will use this Night to rest. When the Sun rises, you will wake up and resume normal activities. When the Sun sets, you will know it's time to go home."

The crowd dispersed, and everyone wondered how this new world with Day and Night would be. The Sun set as planned and it became cooler and cooler, which was a relief to everyone. But then, it also became darker and darker, which terrified one and all. No one could see a thing. There was chaos. That is how the first darkness came to be.

SLOSH! A farmer accidentally stepped into some cow dung and was stuck with smelly shoes.

"OUCH!" yelled a carpenter as a splinter pierced her skin. Blood oozed out, but she couldn't see it, of course.

CRACK! A child broke his wooden horse toy by stepping on it and cried loudly.

The Creator heard the commotion and went rushing to the world below.

"What is wrong now?"

"We can't see anything!" the people cried. "Please bring back the Sun!"

The Creator flipped through some old notes and thought for a little while. Bringing back the Sun wouldn't help. "Should I make a second sun? Perhaps one that will gently glow, not shine?" he wondered.

The Creator waved and a pristine white, glowing, spherical ball appeared in the dark sky which later came to be known as the Moon. People could see each other! They could go home safely without falling, work without stepping into dung, make furniture without getting hurt, and play without breaking their toys.

And the soft, soothing glow that made everyone happy came to be known as Moonlight.

The Sage's Daughter

A story from the Katha Sarit Sagara

The powerful Sage was so deep in meditation that he did not hear the gurgling of the river that flowed next to him. Neither did he hear the soft breeze that blew through the tree where he was sitting, nor the rustle followed by a loud screech. Then, THWACK!

Something soft and small fell into his lap. He opened his eyes and saw a baby mouse, quivering and squealing in fear.

"You are not an animal of the trees or of the sky. How did you fall from above?"

He looked up and saw an eagle gliding, looking this way and that. "Ah," said the Sage with a smile, "you had a lucky escape, little one. Don't worry, you are safe now."

He got up and walked back towards his home, a small hut where he lived with his wife. The little mouse, now cradled against his chest, stopped squealing. The Sage's wife came out when she heard her husband, surprised that he was back early.

As he got closer, she noticed that he was holding something. She smiled when she saw the mouse and as she looked into the little creature's eyes, her heart melted.

"Did you see her family anywhere?" she asked. The Sage shook his head. "Then, perhaps we could keep her as our child for we don't have any of our own?" the wife asked.

The Sage smiled and agreed. He closed his eyes, and chanted a mantra, and the little mouse started changing.

Her whiskers fell away and her pink, pointy ears became smaller. She turned into a little girl, now curled up in the wife's lap. The Sage's wife held her daughter close. She already loved her so much.

The girl grew up to be an independent woman, as learned as her father, quick-witted and intelligent. The Sage wanted her to marry, but knew that the groom had to be someone special, just like her.

"No ordinary man will do for my precious girl. I will find a groom among the great kings," he told his wife.

So he summoned the Sun God. "You are so powerful, you drive away the night," he told him. "Will you marry my daughter?" The Sun God smiled, shining brighter in order to impress the Sage's daughter.

She shrank back, hiding her eyes from the glare. "No father!" she exclaimed. "I cannot marry him. He is mighty and full of fire. His heat will burn me."

The Sage was disappointed, but the Sun God consoled him. "How about the King of Clouds? He does not burn and he is more powerful than me. He can even cloak me whenever he wants to."

The Sage called for the King of Clouds who appeared, dark and gloomy. His voice was a crack of thunder, so loud it shook the ground and bent the trees. The Sage's daughter quivered and hid behind the door. "Not him," she said. "He is too loud. How will I talk to him?"

Perplexed, the Sage looked at the King of Clouds, who thundered, "How about the Wind God? He is mightier than me. He is not as loud as me and can blow me to far-off places."

The Wind God came next, knocking on the Sage's door. But he came as a whirlwind, so fast and terrible that everything – even the roof – flew away. The daughter held on to the door and said, "Not him, father. The Wind God is always travelling great distances. I want to stay in one place and call it home."

"Perhaps the Mountain God?" suggested the Wind God as he blew away. "He is so strong, nothing can move him."

But the Mountain God did not suit either. He was too tall, too coarse, and too distant. No, he would not do at all. The Mountain God saw how upset the Sage was and said:

"Worry not. How about
the King of the Mice?
He is so mighty he can
burrow through the
hardest of surfaces.
Even me!"

And so, the Sage turned to the King of the Mice. The King came to the Sage's home, riding a tiny chariot, wearing a gold crown that gleamed in the sun. He looked at the daughter and bowed, deep and low.

The Sage's daughter bent down and looked into his eyes. His voice was soft and as the two talked it became obvious that he was just as wise as her.

The Sage saw the smile on his daughter's face and knew it was a perfect match.

So, he spoke a mantra and his daughter transformed back into a mouse.

A grand wedding was held
that day for the perfect
couple. And the two lived
happily ever after.

The King and the Parrot
A tale from the Upper North

There once lived a king, wise but a little short-tempered. He had a parrot, unlike any other, with wings speckled with gold.

The parrot and the king were inseparable. She would perch on his shoulder when he travelled across the kingdom, sleep on the softest of silks, and eat the juiciest fruits from the royal garden.

One day, the king noticed that the parrot looked a little sad. Worried, he begged her to tell him what had happened.

She hopped closer to him and said, "Dear king, I have been with you for so many years, but I also miss my home. Let me go for a few months. I promise to return."

The king refused to let her go. But as days passed, he saw the parrot become sadder and quieter. Finally, he gave her permission, but added: "Bring back a token of your love, something that will show me how much you missed me."

She promised him, spread her wings, and flew high into the sky, soaring over green fields and crossing blue seas, until she came to a desert where the sun shone so bright that plants wilted before they even took root.

The parrot flew past the never-ending desert until she came to a river that flowed so fast, not even rocks could stand in its way. On its banks, stood a clump of trees with barely any leaves. Here the parrot built a nest and laid six eggs, all speckled gold. For six months, she lived by the raging river, until it was time to return to her king.

But before flying back, she visited the Garden of the Fairies for the perfect gift for her king, a token of her love. The garden was blooming, for it was always spring here. Butterflies flitted across flowers of every colour and the trees grew tall, their branches touching the clouds. At the edge of the garden was an enchanted tree. The parrot picked two small apples, juicy and deep red.

The parrot flew back to her king and, dropping the apples in his lap, perched on his shoulder. The king was overjoyed. But the time apart had also made him suspicious.

What are these apples, he wondered and, just to be safe, gave one to his dog. The dog bit into the apple gleefully, for it was juicy and sweet. As he ate it, he started choking and died. Furious, the king told his ministers to banish the parrot so that she may never return. He then threw the second apple as far away as possible.

The enchanted apple fell in the furthest corner of the garden. That night, it grew and grew and, by the morning, had become a tree. Its trunk was so wide and thick, no axe could fell it. Its leaves glistened in the sun and the tiny, juicy apples, as red as roses, hung from its branches. It came to be called The Tree of Death for everyone knew what had happened to the king's dog. No one went near it.

Now, in another corner of the garden lived an old couple who were employed at the stables, but had become so old they could no longer work. They had been asked to leave and had nowhere to go. So they picked two apples from The Tree of Death.

"It is better to eat this apple and die rather than be cast out of this place, where we have lived all our life," the old man told the old woman. She agreed and the two ate the apples.

The next morning, as the king walked through his garden, he saw a man and woman standing next to The Tree of Death. Strapping and strong, they looked quite puzzled. The king walked up to the strangers and demanded to know who they were. How had they entered the royal gardens? Where were the guards? He would have them thrown into prison. The couple pleaded for mercy.

"Please, your majesty," the young man said. "We used to work in the stables. We were too old and had nowhere to go. We ate these apples last night because we wanted to die."

The king didn't believe them. So, he called the oldest minister in his cabinet and demanded that he eat an apple from the tree. The minister did what he was told, but was quite nervous. He wasn't ready to die just as yet.

As the king watched, the minister transformed. The years slipped away as the wrinkles on his face disappeared. His hunched back became straight and the quiver in his hand faded.

The king realized that the parrot had truly shared a token of her love with him. *But why did the dog die?* He called the sorcerer who performed a spell and told the king that, unknown to the parrot, a poisonous snake had licked the first apple.

The king knew he had made a mistake. He searched far and wide for his beloved parrot who had been nothing but loyal and loving.

But she was gone, never to be seen again.

Legend of the Glacier-Hearted Queen

A myth from Punjab

Before humans lived on the earth, the kings and queens of the world were planets, great oceans, and mighty mountains.

Now, the king of all the mountains was the handsome Westerwan. He stood at the centre towering over all the other mountains, casting a dark shadow over them. They didn't even get an inch of sunlight. No one was happy about that.

In the winter, Westerwan was covered in a bed of thick snow, pristine white and undisturbed because he was so high up in the clouds. The other mountains, standing in his shadow, were left with dirty brown, muddy slush. At night, he stood in the same stance, but wore a crown made of stars. No one was happy about that either.

Westerwan was also arrogant and looked down on all who were shorter than him, which was everyone. Suffice to say, no one was thrilled about that at ALL!

Among the miserable lot were Haramukh and Nanga Parbat. Every time they sought his audience, Westerwan would pay them no heed. He was too engrossed in his looks.

"Look at him, wearing the clouds as a royal robe," complained Haramukh. "King of the mountains. Pfft! He doesn't deserve the title at all."

Nanga Parbat agreed, "He spends the day and night looking at his reflection in the lakes. What good is he? We need a new ruler. Anyone would do a better job than him!"

Winter passed and spring came. With it, the sun revealed Gwashbrari, the glacier. Icy, quiet, and dignified, she was known through the land for her beauty. Gwashbrari didn't care for anyone towering over her. Others could reach as high as the clouds, but she was the wisest and most alluring in all the land.

Tired of living in Westerwan's shadow, Haramukh, Nanga Parbat, and the other annoyed mountains turned to Gwashbrari to seek her help in defeating their king.

"Why should I care?" she told the disgruntled mountains. "His head may reach the stars, but his feet are on the earth. The same earth we stand on. We are all made of the same matter. He's just made of some extra matter. That is all."

"This is why, we must overthrow him," appealed Haramukh.

"He's so pompous, just because he's the tallest," said Nanga Parbat.

"Who is this Westerwan? He's no king to me. His head may rise as high as the planets. But, I am the real queen," she stated haughtily.

All the mountains burst out laughing. "You are no queen!" exclaimed one, "Look how short you are!"

Gwashbrari ignored them. "You laugh now, but wait and see," she said. "Before tomorrow, Westerwan will be begging me to become his queen."

They sniggered and sneered and turned away. Unperturbed, for she didn't care a bit for what they said, Gwashbrari carried on as if nothing had ever happened.

She smiled through the day and even shrugged off some snow. It landed at her feet with a gentle poof, in a cloud of white powdery smoke.

As the sun started setting and the sky turned a rosy hue, Gwashbrari began to glow against the saffron sky. She glistened, shining brighter than the North Star.

Westerwan was minding his own business, admiring his reflection in the lake, when he saw a radiant sight. It was Gwashbrari in all her glory. He was smitten and, almost immediately, fell in love.

As the sun set lower, Gwashbrari was still as radiant as ever. It was as if she were blushing at the sight of Westerwan, the king of all the mountains.

"Gwashbrari, please come to me," he said. "I think I love you. Where have you been hiding all this while?"

His voice echoed through the valley. Everyone stopped what they were doing and began to listen.

To the world, Gwashbrari blushed, but she was smirking to herself. "Dear king, how is that possible? I am the lowest of them all," she said. "How can I reach you? Or even speak to you. Your face is too high. So high that only the stars can rest on it. Even if I stood on my tiptoes I will not be able to reach your shoulder that is covered by the clouds."

Then, everyone heard the king's passionate plea, "Please come to me, we'll rule together."

"If you love me, you should know that everyone who loves must bow. You must come towards me," she replied.

All the mountains heard a deep rumble. Their proud king was inching towards Gwashbrari. They couldn't believe their eyes. The ground began to shake and cracks began to form. Now scared, all the mountains held on to each other. Forgetting his pride and ego, Westerwan began moving towards his beloved, causing a quake.

The sun finally set and Gwashbrari's rosy blush faded. She stood motionless with a slight smile, as cold as ice.

Then, the moon rose and
the stars appeared. The mighty
king of all the mountains
had fallen at her feet.
Westerwan no longer
wore his crown.

The Chatty Wooden Legs

A tale from Eastern India

In a quiet little village, at the edge of four forests, each deeper and denser than the other, lived a polite young man and his wife. They were always courteous and ready to help. The man was a bit useless, though, the villagers would say, as he hadn't worked a single day in his life. It didn't matter, really, because his parents had left him money, enough to live happily. Until one day the money started running out.

"Don't worry," the man told his wife. The next day, he picked up a big axe with a long handle that always stood by his door, and walked into the first forest. He saw a tall tree that looked quite old, stopped and bowed.

Now it's important to remember that all trees have spirits living in them. They are mostly generous and kind, but can also be quite moody. So it is always best to be polite. The man certainly did not want to displease the spirits, so he asked, in as cordial a tone as possible, "Tree, tree, may I cut you down?" The tree ignored him.

He walked through the entire forest asking as politely as he could, but never got an answer. As the sun set, he returned home.

The next morning, the man grabbed his axe and walked into the second forest. He stopped when he spotted a tall tree with branches that reached towards the sky.

"Tree, tree, may I cut you down?" he asked. The tree didn't say a word. So, he walked to the next tree, and then the next, and then the next. He crossed the entire forest, but returned empty-handed.

The third morning, the man walked into the third forest and was met with complete silence once again. Not a single tree would talk to him. The wife did not say anything when he returned, but her brow was furrowed. That night, for the first time in a long, long time, they ate dinner in silence, each worried about the future.

The fourth day dawned bright and sunny, just like the other three days. The man picked up his axe and walked out of the door. This forest was the furthest of them all, right at the very edge of the village. It was darker and denser, and its trees were older than the village. The man walked till he reached the centre and then asked a mango tree, gnarled and twisted. "Tree, tree, may I cut you down?"

The spirit in this mango tree had lived many moons and had heard of this polite young man. He wanted to help.

"Yes, you may," the spirit replied in a voice that rustled like the breeze playing with the leaves.

And so, the man cut the tree as politely as he could and took the wood home. Now his wife, who had been patient all this while, nearly snapped at him, when she saw the wood.

What in the world will he do with a tree, she wondered, quite angry, truth be told. Then the man said, "I am going to build a bed, unlike you have ever seen. Don't disturb me for a week."

For seven days and seven nights, the house echoed with sawing and chopping, hammering and banging. Then, on the eighth day, the bed was ready. The wife's mouth fell open in surprise, for it really was unlike anything she had ever seen.

The bed had carvings of the forest with leaves and flowers, birds, and animals that almost looked real. But, it had odd legs. Each was a curious face with a pointy beard.

The man tied the bed to a cart and took it to a city many miles away. He went to the market and a crowd collected. Everyone wanted the bed. "Name your price," the merchants shouted, but the man shook his head. He waited. Soon, news of this extraordinary bed reached the king who lived in a palace with many rooms. Curious, he ordered his guards to bring the man and the bed.

One look and the king knew he had to have it. He paid the man a handsome amount and sent him on his way. As the man left, he told the king, in a rather cryptic tone, "Tonight, when you get into bed, do not sleep. You will hear something important."

That night, the king climbed into the bed and tucked himself in. He tried not to sleep, which was difficult because the bed was really, really comfortable. The king waited and waited. Then, just as he felt his eyes closing, he heard squeaks and felt a bump, as if the bed were adjusting itself. He peered over the edge of the bed and saw the bed's legs talking to each other.

"Hey, I am tired of holding the bed up," one leg said. "I want to see the king's courtyard. Stand firm till I return." So saying, it hopped out of the door and made its way to the palace courtyard. There, it spotted two snakes arguing.

"I am going to bite the king," one snake said.

"No, I am," the other hissed back. The first snake shook its head and said, "No, I am. I am going to hide in his shoe and bite him."

The leg hopped back to the king's chamber and told the other legs what it had seen. "The king better check his shoes, if he doesn't want to get bitten," it said.

The second leg stretched and said, "Hold the bed up. I want to see the king's garden. Stand firm till I return." It hopped all the way to the edge of the garden to the abandoned old palace with a lopsided roof.

The wind was busy singing to itself as it made its way through the broken open windows when it saw the leg. "This roof is going to fall and hurt someone," it said breezily.

The leg hopped back and told the other legs what he had seen. "Hmm," the legs creaked. "The king better get the roof fixed if he doesn't want people to get hurt."

The third leg, quite tired of standing around, told the other legs that it was going to the city. "Stand firm till I return," it said and hopped across the courtyard and the garden, past the palace gates, and into the city. It stopped when it came across four men whispering. They were planning to rob the king's treasury.

The leg returned and told the other legs what it had seen and heard. "If the king is smart, he will have guards waiting for them in the treasury," the third leg said as it took its place.

Hearing this, the king started to get out of bed, when the fourth leg creaked. It wanted an adventure of its own. "Stand firm till I return," it said and hopped off to explore the forest outside the city. As it wandered through the trees, the leg heard voices and spotted a band of dacoits sitting around a fire. A young girl was tied to the tree. It was the princess, the king's daughter!

The leg returned to the palace and told the other legs what it had seen. "If the king hurries," it said, "he will catch the dacoits and rescue his daughter."

The king leapt out of bed. First, he shook his shoes well. A snake popped out and slithered away. The king realized that the legs were telling the truth. Then, he grabbed his sword and ran down the hall calling for the guards and his horse. As he jumped on to his horse, he sent a group of guards to the treasury, just in case.

Riding as fast as he could, the king and his guards rushed through the forest and to the clearing. There, he saw his daughter tied to the tree. The dacoits, who weren't expecting the king, were caught red-handed and the princess was rescued.

Back at the palace, the king sat down to catch his breath. The night had been a little too hectic and he hadn't slept at all. That's when he spotted the palace architect and sent him to repair the old palace. Good thing too, because the architect told him that the roof would have fallen and injured the gardeners working nearby. Of course, the guards hiding in the treasury caught the thieves who had climbed over the wall to steal the king's money.

The talkative legs had saved the king, his daughter, and the kingdom. So, there was only one thing left to do. The king called for the polite young man who had built the bed. He gave him so much money that the man would never have to work another day in his life.

And what of the chatty legs?
Well, ever so often, they would get
bored of standing firm and travel the
kingdom, bringing back stories of what
they had seen and heard.

How Hanuman Nearly Ate the Sun

A story from the Kishkindha Kandam

The Sun stretched and sighed and with every stretch and sigh, rays of light lit up each corner of the sky, bouncing across the blue, turning him into a bright, yellowish orange ball of warmth and heat.

Far, far below, on Earth, in a dense green forest, a baby monkey searched for food. His stomach grumbled and growled, but there were no fruits or berries to be found. As he climbed the tallest tree in the forest, reaching its very tip, he looked around and up at the sky.

"Wait! What is that?" he thought
spotting the Sun that glowed so fiercely.
"Is that a ripe fruit?"

His mother, Anjana had told him: "If you are hungry, look for bananas, mangoes, and berries. You will know the ripest, juiciest one by the colour of its skin. It could be red, a bright yellow and, sometimes, even orange."

The little monkey sat on the branch of the tallest tree and pondered, blinking his big brown eyes. That does indeed look like a ripe, juicy fruit, he thought, looking at the Sun.

There was only one thing to do. He leapt for the sky, one hand stretched out towards the Sun, all the better to grab it.

The Sun was minding his own business, when he looked down at Earth and spotted a tiny figure, flying up towards the skies, pushing aside the clouds, one arm stretched out towards him.

He laughed, deep and rumbling. "What a silly little child," the Sun muttered as he stretched, burning brighter, becoming a little more orange. The laughter ended in a rather abrupt, ungodly squeak.

"Wait… wait," the mighty Sun whimpered. "Why… How… is he coming at me so fast. Help!" So saying, he scrambled across the sky, trying to escape the determined little monkey.

The little monkey was really hungry now but the Sun seemed to be moving away. So he sped up a little, entering Space. It was all quiet here. There were just the planets and the stars, the comets and the galaxies.

The little one was not interested in icy, cold planets. The warmth of the Sun beckoned. He gently pushed the planets out of his way and focused on the Sun, who seemed to be trembling a bit.

The Sun looked around and spotted Indra, the God of all Gods, and waved to catch his attention. Indra saw the Sun looking rattled and quite anxious, and went over.

"Help, Indra, help. That little monkey is racing towards me. It looks like he is going to eat me," the Sun cried. Even as he said these words, the monkey seemed to be inching closer. The Sun tried to hide behind Indra. "Help. Help," he pleaded. The Sun was definitely trembling now.

Indra grew alarmed. The little monkey was rapidly approaching and it almost seemed like he was charging at the Sun. Was he a demon child, Indra wondered. *How dare he attack the almighty Sun!*

Indra felt a rage grow inside him. Before he knew it, he had taken a deep breath and thrown a lightning bolt at the monkey.

The bolt cut through Space and hit the little one on his jaw, throwing him off balance and knocking him unconscious. The little monkey fell, shooting past the planets and stars and landing on a mountaintop still and lifeless.

Far away, Vayu, the Wind god, heard the crackle of thunder and the sharp whiz of a lightning bolt. His heart sank. Something bad had happened. He rushed towards the sound and saw the little monkey lying on a mountain, still.

With a loud roar that shook the clouds and pierced through the mountains, Vayu rushed to pick up the little monkey, his beloved, little son Anjaneya. His grief gave way to anger when he saw Indra, who realized that he had made a grave mistake.

"How dare you," thundered Vayu. "How dare you hurt my son! Now, you will pay the price for wounding an innocent child."

So saying, Vayu picked up his son and walked into a cave, never-ending and dark. A boulder rolled across the opening, closing them off to the outside world.

There was panic across Earth and Heaven. The wind stopped blowing and everything grew still. Vayu had withdrawn from the world and in doing so had taken the air with him.

No one could breathe. Not the gods, nor the birds and animals, trees and insects.

Indra fell to his knees and prayed to Brahma, the creator of all that is and all that will be. Only he could save the world now. "O Brahma, help me," he pleaded, when he felt a hand on his shoulder. It was Brahma. He smiled and transported both of them to the cave.

Indra saw Vayu sitting in a corner holding his son. He knelt down and folded his hands in an apology. He caressed the baby's face, his heart melting at its innocence.

Suddenly, the little one opened his eyes. He was alive! The thunderbolt had barely hurt him, just injured his jaw.

Impressed by the little monkey's power and agility, both the gods gave him several boons. Brahma smiled as he said, "No weapon will ever harm you."

"Your death shall take place according to your will," promised Indra.

Placated, Vayu came out of the cave and the universe breathed once again. The birds chirped and the flowers bloomed.

And what of the little one?
He came to be known as
Hanuman, the monkey god
who nearly ate the Sun.

The Secret Keeper

An oral tale from across India

A very long time ago there was a king, taller than many and shorter than a few. But what set him apart were his ears – long and straight with a mind of their own. They flopped this way and that, like those of a donkey, much to the king's despair.

They had been this way ever since he had taken a magic potion for perfect ears. Something had gone wrong and now, he was stuck with ears so long they did not fit under any crown or hat. So, he had to wrap a long, narrow piece of cloth around them, like a turban. It was the oddest headgear the kingdom had ever seen, so tall, the king had to bend to walk through doors.

Of course, no one in the kingdom knew they were this long. *It was a royal secret.*

One morning, the king looked into the mirror, saw his ears, and tried to ignore the little whisper of fear. He was going to share his secret, for the first time, with the royal barber. He didn't have a choice. His hair had become so long that the ministers had stopped taking him seriously. All they did was giggle, even when he tried to discuss something serious like taxes.

There was a gentle tap on the door. "Come," the king roared, sounding grumpier than usual.

The barber shuffled into the empty royal chamber and saw the king glaring at him. His knees shook and his voice trembled as he bowed low and said, "Your majesty, you called for me."

"Yes," the king thundered. "Cut my hair."

The barber gulped and walked up to the king. His hands shook as he opened his kit. "Y-y-your turban," he said. The king's eyes narrowed.

The barber squeaked as the king glared at him as if he would eat him or throw him to the tigers.

"Before you begin, you must promise," the king commanded. "Whatever you see here, you will never tell any human. Else, you will spend the rest of your life in prison." The barber nodded, his eyes wide with fear.

Then, the king unwrapped the turban. Round and round, until POP! His ears sprang free.

The barber gasped, but looked away when the king growled. Wiping the sweat off his brow, he started trimming the king's hair, trying to ignore the ears that flipped this way and that. Once done, he grabbed a purse full of gold coins that the king handed him, and ran home. The next month, the barber cut the king's hair once again, hands trembling, almost in tears, trying not to look at the long ears. And so it went on every month.

The secret started taking a toll. The barber stopped sleeping. He was petrified that he would reveal the secret without meaning to. He even stopped talking to his wife. Instead, he would sit in a corner at home looking at the wall, dreading the next visit to the palace. This continued for months. Finally, his wife couldn't take it any longer.

"What is the matter?" she asked. At first, the barber refused to speak, but after much coaxing, said, "I have a secret. But, I can't tell you. I can't tell anyone. I made a promise. What should I do? *What should I do?*"

His wife was silent for a while and then said, "You must never break a promise, so you can never tell a human. But you should lighten your mind. Why don't you tell a tree?"

The barber liked the idea. There was no harm in telling a tree. So, the next day, he walked to the nearest jungle and searched for the perfect secret keeper. It was a shisham tree with a small hollow. Cupping his hands around it, he whispered:

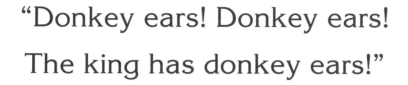

"Donkey ears! Donkey ears!
The king has donkey ears!"

He started feeling better almost right away. So, every month, on his way back home from the royal haircut, he would go to the tree and whisper:

"Donkey ears! Donkey ears!
The king has donkey ears!"

With every visit, the shisham tree absorbed the barber's whispered words, becoming bigger and bigger.

Then, one day, a tabla player saw the tree. It was now tall and gleaming because of the king's secret. The musician thought it would make the perfect tabla for the annual royal music festival.

The day of the festival dawned and people came from across the realm. There was a scent of marigold in the air. The barber sat in the front row wearing his best outfit. The king wore a special tall turban with gold spangles.

The musician walked on to the stage carrying a tabla, which he placed on the carpet. The minister in charge of music stood up and said, "Made from the finest shisham tree, this tabla's music will make you dance."

The tabla maestro tapped the tabla and started playing. But there were no beats. Instead, it sang out, loud and clear:

"Don-key e-ars! Don-key e-ars! The king has don-key e-ars!"

Everyone fell silent. The king jumped up, his face red, turban swaying.

The tabla player gulped and tried once again.

"Don-key e-ars... Don-key e-ars... The ki-ng has don-key e-ars!"

the tabla sang out.

The king looked around and saw the barber trying to hide under his chair.

"YOU!" the king shouted, pointing at the barber and the guards grabbed him. "I-I've been I-loyal, your majesty. I never said a word to another human," the barber stammered.

Frustrated, the king growled and pulled off the turban, threw it on the ground, and stomped on it. The audience gasped as his ears, now free, flipped and flopped. Then, someone giggled and before the king could do anything, the entire hall started laughing.

The barber wailed. "I promise, your majesty. I told no one. I only told a tree. A shisham tree."

The king stopped kicking the turban and looked at the barber. Then, he looked at the tabla maestro, who was muttering. "This was the finest shisham tree in the forest. I don't understand."

Finally, the king understood. He slumped in his throne and looked around. His subjects were laughing, some were rolling on the floor while others were sitting there, shocked. The secret was out.

Then, something amazing happened. For the first time in his life, the king felt free. He smiled to himself.

He no longer had to hide who he was. At last, he was happy.

Journey to Heaven

A story from Eastern India

There was once a farmer with a fondness for bright, colourful turbans who had a hare-brained idea. "What if I grew fried corn in my field? Wouldn't that be nice? I could sprinkle some salt and pepper and eat it straight from the cob. Maybe squeeze a lime. That would be delicious," he wondered out loud.

Pleased with his plan, he went to his field the very next day with perfectly fried corn kernels. He sowed them one by one, placed the spookiest scarecrow right in the centre, admired his handiwork, and returned home.

Unknown to him, every night at 12, an elephant descended from heaven on to the fields in the village. He would eat fresh harvest, leaving behind large, round footprints. That night, the elephant made for the farmer's field, polished off the harvest, and trampled all over his newly planted fried corn.

The following day, the farmer wore his finest turban and went to the field. It was a mess! There were massive holes all over. The scarecrow was headless, its squashed head lay in a corner.

"It must have been the other farmers," he exclaimed. "They must be jealous of my brilliant idea and destroyed my crop." So, the next day, he told anyone who would listen that he was planting fried corn again. Then, at night, he hid and waited to catch the criminal in the act.

Darkness fell, the stars came out, and a crescent moon was smiling. The farmer dozed off, when BANG! He woke up with a start and saw a bright light shining from the sky. Then a white elephant descended, landing on his neighbour's farm.

The elephant pulled corn ears with his trunk, shoved them into his mouth, stomped all over, and left massive footprints. Once he was full, he leapt towards the sky. Curious to see where he was going, the farmer ran after him and grabbed his tail.

Up, up, up, the elephant flew for he belonged to the god of heaven.

In heaven, a carnival was in full swing. The god sat on his throne, surrounded by magical beings. The farmer slipped into the crowd, but the god spotted his large turban and called him over.

"How did you enter my kingdom?" he asked. The farmer's palms became sweaty as he stammered, "Umm … Your highness, your heavenly elephant destroyed my crops and I followed him here."

"Is that true?" the god asked looking at the white elephant sternly. He smiled innocently. "I am sorry for the trouble," the god said. "I love your turban. Such beautiful colours and wrapped so precisely. I'd like to buy it," he said, and pulled out a bag full of celestial gold coins!

The farmer happily handed him the turban and took the bag. Then, with the snap of the god's fingers, he was home. The first thing he did was show his friends and neighbours the gold coins. Soon the entire village knew. They all wanted to go to heaven and get rich. The farmer promised to take them.

The next night the farmer and the other villagers waited in the fields. At the stroke of midnight, the elephant descended on to a field.

Chomp, chomp, chomp. He ate with abandon leaving behind empty corn leaves.

Stomp, stomp, stomp. He trampled all over leaving giant, round footprints.

Then, once his tummy was full, he leapt for the sky. The farmer gave a signal and caught the elephant's tail, holding on tightly. One of his neighbours grabbed his leg. Slowly, one-by-one they grabbed each other's legs forming a human chain.

Up, Up, Up, they went.

As they flew through the night sky, the farmer told the others about the carnival and the god who bought his colourful turban.

"You won't believe it," he said, clutching the elephant's tail. "The most delicious dishes were served, the kind you would never see back home. They just melted in my mouth as I took a bite out of them!"

"Tell us more. Tell us more," his neighbours begged.

"Then, the god of heaven called me to his court. He really liked my turban. I wore it the same way yesterday, just a little less extravagant. He said he'd never seen such a style. 'It's so huge', he said. Then, he wanted to buy my turban! Can you believe it? I couldn't," he yelled down to his neighbours.

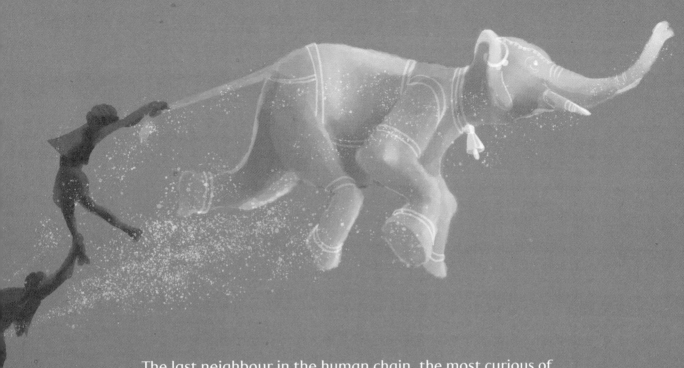

The last neighbour in the human chain, the most curious of them all, yelled back, "Exactly how long was your turban again?"

Without thinking, the farmer let go of the elephant's tail, stretching out his hands to demonstrate the length of the turban. "This big," he managed to say before he realized he was falling, as were the others.

Down, down, down.

They fell past the stars and the clouds. Then, with a loud thud, they landed on a bed of haystacks in a jumbled heap. The farmer, of course, fell on top of all of them with his turban intact. Annoyed, the neighbours grumbled and limped home.

That day the farmer learnt an important lesson – to always think before acting.

As for the celestial elephant, he always checked his tail for passengers before taking off for heaven.

The Cursed King

A legend from the Rajatarangini

Once upon a time, a man named Damodara ruled Kashmir. A kind and benevolent king, he did everything he could in his power for his people.

Like the time he sought the help of his friend, Kuber, the god of wealth, to build a dam for Damodarasuda, a town named after him. Built on an elevated plateau, the barren and rocky town had no water. So, on his request, Kuber asked his magical attendants, the Guhyakas, to build a dam. They made it in a week! Had humans constructed it, it would have taken decades.

The people of the town were thoroughly impressed with their king. "What a great man," they would say while admiring the dam. "Nothing is impossible for King Damodara!"

Aside from his great deeds, the king was known to be a rigid man with a strict routine. He also had a temper, which flared up from time to time.

One day, the king and some of his ministers were passing through Damodarasuda on their way to the Vitasta river for a royal bath. All of a sudden his carriage stopped. The ministers stepped out to check and returned to tell him: "Sir, there are five sages and they wish to meet you."

The king got out of his carriage and walked towards them. Why on earth would they halt my journey, he wondered.

Now, these sages were quite notorious. They were known across the lands for their magical powers and expected everyone to do exactly as they commanded.

The sages saw the king, and said, "We are tired from our long journey. Please give us some food."

"I can only offer you food once I have bathed in the Vitasta. Please wait," the king replied politely.

"Why do you want to go all the way to the river, when we can bring it here," said one of the sages and waved his hand. At once, the Vitasta appeared, flowing past the king's carriage.

"Here, you have your river. Now give us food," demanded one of the sages.

The king gasped looking at the river. "This is nothing but an illusion," he thought. "These sages are trying to fool me and keep me from my holy bath." This angered him. The king screamed at the sages, "What is this sorcery? Begone at once!"

The sages were astonished that instead of following their command, the king had shouted at them. Angry, they turned on him:

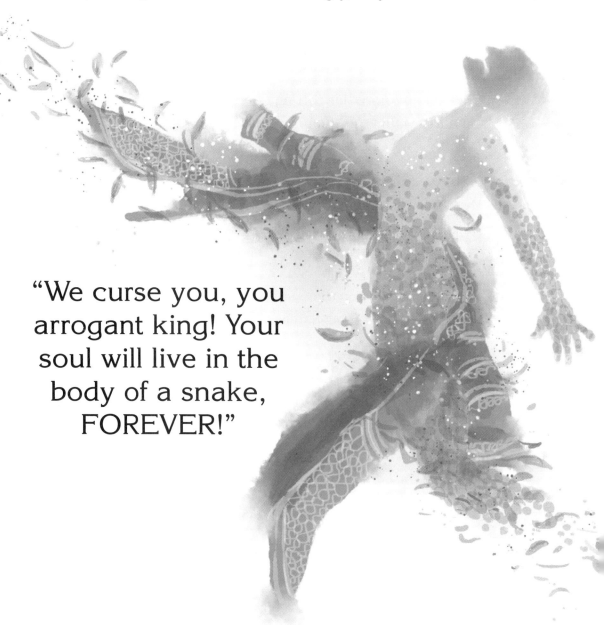

"We curse you, you arrogant king! Your soul will live in the body of a snake, FOREVER!"

Together, they clenched their teeth, pointed, and glared at the him. A whirlwind surrounded the king, as he rose in the air, dry leaves and dust encircled him. His robes blew away in tatters and his skin started turning into the slippery scales of a snake.

Before the ministers could react, a pile of royal clothes lay where, just a moment ago, the king had stood. A snake slithered out from the bundle.

Stunned, the ministers ran to the sages and fell to their knees, "Please give us back our king! Take back your curse, we beg you."

The sages replied in unison: "We won't take it back. What is done is done. But, we can bind it with time. This curse will only be lifted after your king finds a person who will, willingly and patiently, sit with him and read the entire Ramayana. Only then will the curse end, and your king will become a human again."

The sages laughed as they walked away. The shocked ministers were left standing as their king slithered away from their sight!

It is rumoured that, even today, King Damodara roams Damodarasuda and Kashmir in his snake form, hissing and searching for people who will recite the Ramayana to him.

But, of course, he could really be anywhere.

How to Fool a Bhoota
A Tamil tale

The wind sighed as it made its way through the palm trees and heard voices, raised and irritable. They are at it again, so thinking, it continued on its way. But Vayalvallan and Kaiyalvallan did not. Instead, they stopped right there at the crossroads and continued their argument.

"My words are like magic," said Vayalvallan, he who is Mighty-of-the-Mouth. "So I am better."

"Nothing can match the power of my hands," snorted Kaiyalvallan, he who is Mighty-of-the-Hands.

"I can convince people of anything with mere words."

"I can lift anything, no matter how heavy it is."

"Words are stronger."

"No, hands are."

And so they went on, until the sun set, darkness fell, and Vayalvallan's little daughter came looking for her father. There was no way to solve this, they realized. So, the two friends decided to live together until they had solved their dilemma. Days turned into months, but the problem remained unsolved. Who was truly better? Was it Mighty-of-the-Mouth or Mighty-of-the-Hands? Was it Vayalvallan or Kaiyalvallan?

Finally, it was the festival season. Every year, for nine days, villagers stopped working and celebrated. They feasted, danced, welcomed their neighbours into their homes, and made merry. So too did Vayalvallan and Kaiyalvallan. But something was missing.

"A goat!" said Kaiyalvallan. "That's what is missing. We need to make goat curry for our guests." Then, he winked at his friend and said, "But since we are mighty, let's steal a goat from the field next door." Vayalvallan chuckled and agreed.

That night the two friends snuck out of their homes (for if their wives had discovered what they were up to, they would have most certainly put a stop to this nonsense).

They hid behind the bushes that bordered the field next door. As they watched, the shepherd guarding the goats, stuck a long, wooden staff into the ground and covered it with a blanket. From a distance, it looked like a small sleeping boy. Then, they heard the shepherd say loudly, just in case anyone was listening, "Son, I am off to eat my dinner. Guard this place well. There are many tigers and bhootas-kootas. They should not steal our goats."

Now, kootas don't really exist; the shepherd enjoyed speaking in rhymes. But bhootas, or goblins, do exist and one entered the field at that very moment looking to make a plump goat his meal. A little taller than the average goblin, but not as smart, with pointy teeth and sharp claws, this bhoota was terribly hungry. He stopped when he heard the shepherd.

"What were kootas?" he wondered aloud, shuddering, for he had never heard of such creatures. "Maybe they are bigger than us, with sharper teeth. Maybe they are more powerful." The bhoota quaked at the thought of fearsome kootas, when he heard a thump. Not wanting to be eaten, the bhoota quickly turned himself into a plump, little goat.

"Shh," said Kaiyalvallan when he heard the thump, for it was Vayalvallan who did not quite know how to be sneaky. "There is a little boy sleeping over there." Vayalvallan laughed quietly and whispered:

"It's not a boy. That shepherd was crafty. It's just a stick with a blanket on it, made to look like a boy." Kaiyalvallan felt a little silly for being fooled so easily and grunted. The two then started checking the goats, looking for the plumpest one.

The bhoota quivered when he heard the whispers and then the grunt. "Was it the kootas?" it wondered. A pair of hands suddenly picked him up and a voice, that sounded quite like what a koota would, said, "This one is the plumpest of them all."

So saying, Kaiyalvallan picked up the bhoota-goat and put it around his neck. The bhoota-goat was now sure that the kootas were going to cook and eat him. He used a little magic to try and escape.

Kaiyalvallan felt a shudder down his spine and his arms started hurting. "Vayalvallan, I don't know what is happening. This goat is shuddering and shaking and my hands are hurting. This seems to be a magical creature."

Vayalvallan got a little scared when he heard this, but wanting to appear brave, told his friend, "Let's cut the goat in two so that both of us can carry it." The bhoota-goat heard this and started squealing. He whispered a magic spell and disappeared so suddenly that Vayalvallan and Kaiyalvallan shrieked in fear and ran all the way home.

The bhoota flew straight to the banyan tree where he lived with his friends. First, he thanked the bhoota god for his lucky escape and then told his friends about the two fearsome kootas who had captured him.

The other goblins laughed. "You were fooled. Kootas do not exist. Those were humans," they said. But the scared bhoota refused to believe them. "I will show you," he said. "I will take you to their home and you will see how terrible they are."

So the next night, the scared bhoota took the other goblins to Vayalvallan and Kaiyalvallan's home. He warned his friends to be careful, but refused to go anywhere near the house. The other bhootas laughed at him and ignored the warning.

Some bhootas entered the verandah while others stood near the entrance and the back door. Kaiyalvallan was a light sleeper and woke up to see the bhootas standing all around. Scared, he tiptoed into the house and shook Vayalvallan awake. "There are bhootas everywhere. What should we do? We will be eaten," he said. Vayalvallan calmed him down and told him to go back outside and sleep. Then, he woke up his wife.

"There are bhootas outside our home, but don't worry. I have a plan," he told her.

The bhootas saw Kaiyalvallan come back out and go to sleep as if nothing had happened. He didn't seem scared at all. They peered through the window and saw Vayalvallan sitting down to dinner with his wife.

Vayalvallan's wife laid out a palm leaf and water for her husband, then served him some rice and rasam. "Is this all there is?" he growled. "I am really hungry. Where are the three bhootas our son caught on his way back from school? They will make a good meal."

She sighed and said, "Our naughty son wanted some sweets. When I told him there were none, he ate up all the bhootas. What am I to do?"

The bhootas outside the window squealed when they heard this. "If the son eats bhootas for sweets, what would the father do?" one said to the other.

"Eeeee," the bhootas screamed flying back to their friend. "We must leave this place."

"These kootas are dangerous. They will eat us all."

And so the bhootas left their banyan tree and fled to the darkest corner of a nearby forest. They only emerged at night to hunt for food and always with torches that burnt bright.

So it continued for a few months, until one day, Vayalvallan and Kaiyalvallan decided to take a shortcut through that very forest. Night fell as they walked and they decided to stop and sleep in a tree. As they were about to fall asleep, Kaiyalvallan looked down and saw the big group of bhootas carrying torches.

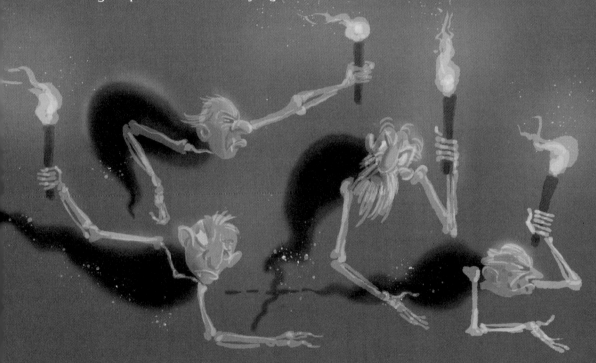

Scared he held on to the branch. But he was trembling so much, he slipped and fell right on top of the bhootas.

Quick-witted Vayalvallan wasted no time. He shouted down, in the loudest voice possible, "Oh Kaiyalvallan, I told you to let those bhootas go. You never listen to me. If you are so hungry that you have to jump on the bhootas, at least catch the meatiest one, so that we may share him."

Now, the bhootas had nearly jumped out of their skin when Kaiyalvallan fell on them. Then, they heard Vayalvallan's deep voice, so terrifying and familiar. This was the same mighty koota, whose son had eaten three bhootas for dessert! They wailed and screamed in fear, dropped the torches, and flew far, far away, never to be seen again.

And Kaiyalvallan had to finally accept that quick-thinking Vayalvallan was indeed the mightiest of them all.

Hare Mark on the Moon

A Jataka tale

Along, long time ago, all the animals in the world could talk. They didn't just speak to one another but to humans as well. Back then, everyone lived in and around a deep forest. In the greenest part of the woodlands lived four best friends – Monkey, Jackal, Otter, and Hare.

Their homes were surrounded by delicate ferns, long grass, and sky-high trees that bore fruits of all kinds – apples, mangoes, bananas, oranges, and many, many more. A stream, brimming with fish, gushed through the woods. A part of the forest was under the shadow of dark and massive mountains where no one ever went. And on the other side was a village full of people who minded their own business.

Monkey, Jackal, Otter, and Hare would meet every evening in a forest clearing. They would talk about their day, crack jokes, play games, and do everything best friends usually do together. When the sun would set, they would go back to their own homes for dinner.

Otter, who lived by the river, would dive into the water and search for juicy, succulent fish.

Monkey, whose home was on the trees, would climb up high to pluck the ripest of fruits.

Jackal, who stayed on the forest floor, would hide behind the trees, stealthily hunt small mammals, and feast on their flesh.

Hare's home was a burrow right next to a meadow. So he would dine on emerald-coloured grass. The brighter it was, the better it tasted.

One evening, Hare noticed that the moon was almost full. Every full moon night, the humans in the village would fast and keep aside some of the tastiest delicacies for anyone who knocked on their door in search of food.

While hopping back home, Hare saw many people crossing the forest. They were carrying fruits, vegetables, and spices to prepare meals for the less fortunate.

Realizing that he was blessed and surrounded by vast green patches of grass, he had an idea. He wondered if his friends would agree.

The next evening, Jackal, Monkey, and Otter were chasing after butterflies. Hare was still deep in thought, wondering about the full moon festival. Thunk! An acorn fell on his head, and distracted him from his thoughts. "Ouch," he exclaimed.

"Are you feeling okay today?" enquired Monkey.

"You look lost," said a concerned Jackal.

"What are you thinking about?" asked Otter.

So, Hare sat down with his four friends and had a heart-to-heart, "We are so lucky. We have the best of fruit, freshest fish, juiciest meat, and grass everywhere. Why don't we fast like the humans? Then we can give the gift of food to those who don't have any."

It made sense to the others. "That's a lovely idea, let's do this," they said together.

And so, the four friends returned home to gather food. This time, they needed to collect enough to share with their visitors.

Otter dived deeper into the stream in search of the largest fish. Jackal took longer than usual and waited for the plumpest mammal with the sweetest meat. And Monkey climbed even higher to pick the most succulent, ripe mangoes. Everyone had the finest and tastiest offerings, except Hare, who was having some trouble. He was dejected and still deep in thought.

He brooded: "I eat grass. Humans do not. I can't hunt small animals, catch fish from the river stream, or climb tall trees. If anyone asks me for food, grass would be of no use to them. Why did I suggest this to my friends? I am the only one that has nothing to give. I feel so embarrassed."

Saddened by his lack of hunting and gathering abilities, he got ready for bed. Then he had another idea, "If anyone comes knocking, maybe I could offer myself as food?" Hare liked the thought of that and had a good night's sleep.

Far up north, up above the clouds, lived Sakra, the ruler of heaven. Every time an act or attempt of true sacrifice took place on earth, the throne of Sakra became warm. This happened the moment the hare thought to give himself up for charity.

Curious, Sakra looked down through the clouds and spotted the long-eared being. *Who was this courageous hare?* He had to find out. The next day, he disguised himself as an old man in tattered clothes leaning on a wobbly wooden cane, and made his way to the forest where the four friends lived.

That same evening, under the shining stars and the soothing light of the full moon, Otter, Monkey, Jackal, and Hare broke their fast together and went home to receive anyone who was in search of alms.

Sakra went to Otter first, who offered him fish. Next, he went to Jackal, who presented him with meat and then to Monkey, who gave him mangoes. Finally, he walked towards the burrow in the meadow to the last of the four friends.

On seeing the old man, Hare was overwhelmed. "Thank you for coming to my home, wise sir," he said. "Today, I will offer you something that I have never given before. There are some logs of wood outside. Please prepare a fire and tell me when it's ready."

Sakra, followed Hare's instructions. Fifteen minutes passed and he spoke, "Dear Hare, everything is ready."

Then Hare stepped into the fire. The yellow and orange flames swirled all around and engulfed him. But the fire didn't burn him, for they were cold. Confused by what had just happened, Hare asked, "What does this mean? Why is this happening? The fire is supposed to cook me, so that you can eat me."

Sakra smiled and revealed his true form. "You are a brave, kind, and selfless creature. Everyone for the rest of eternity will be reminded of your exceptional sacrifice."

So saying, he grabbed one of the shadowy mountains and squeezed black ink out of it. He then reached out to the moon and drew an outline of Hare on its surface. Overcome with emotion, Hare bowed and Sakra went back to heaven.

The mark on the moon was left for everyone in the world to see, to remind them of Hare's kind nature.

As for Hare, he lived happily ever after with his friends who celebrated him every full moon. And it is said, many years later, in another lifetime, unknown to them all, the soul of the fearless and virtuous Hare was reborn as Buddha, the founder of Buddhism.

The Bulbul's Song

A story from Uttar Pradesh

Once a pudgy, little bulbul flew frantically from tree to tree, in search of a perfect one to call his home, for all the ones in his area were either too crowded or too noisy.

Now, this bulbul was on the lookout for a tree that had the juiciest and sweetest fruit, and he wanted it all to himself. This bulbul had many demands.

First, he flew to a jamun tree. Every single branch was occupied by birds. He told himself, "This won't do, this tree has no wing room!"

Then, he spotted a neem tree. It was far too tall and he was too lazy. He said loudly, "No, I don't want to fly that high."

Next, he found a peepul tree with a lot of fruit. He flew towards it and gobbled up the round fruit. Immediately, he spat it out in disgust and yelled, "This is bland! This is not a fruit!"

It is fair to say that this bulbul was very picky and finicky. He found something wrong with every single tree. They were either too slippery to make a nest, not green enough, too high, or just had terrible, tasteless fruit.

Tired and thirsty, the fussy bulbul took a break by a lake. As luck would have it, after taking a gulp of water, he spotted a stumpy tree with a broad trunk. It had bright green leaves, sturdy branches, and bulbs of fruit, which looked delicious. The bulbul fluttered up to the tree. He looked at the bulbs of fruit and chirped in glee. The best part was that it was free of birds.

"This will be my home, I will wait till this fruit is ripe," he declared. "The other birds are so silly. They don't know what they are missing!"

So, the bulbul settled into the tree. He refused to eat or hunt for worms. All he wanted was the fruit. Every day he waited, singing to himself: "First comes the bud, then the flower, and then the fruit, which I will devour."

But the fruits stayed cradled in their buds. "This must be a very special fruit," the bulbul thought, "I wonder why it's taking so long to ripen?"

As time passed, the once plump bird grew weary, but remained determined. He hadn't eaten anything in all this time.

Every time a bird flew past the tree, the bulbul would let out an angry squawk. If they dared to build a home on his tree, he would pick a fight. He would screech, flap his wings, and shout: "Get away from here. This fruit is mine."

Then one day, the buds started opening. The bulbul hopped from branch to branch, checking each one. They turned into beautiful, bright crimson flowers. He ecstatically sang: "First comes the bud, then the flower, AND THEN THE FRUIT, WHICH I WILL DEVOUR!"

Now, a cuckoo who lived nearby was fed up of the bulbul's antics. After seeing the bulbul shoo away yet another bird, she flew to him and said, "This tree doesn't belong to you. You can't make everyone go away."

Weary and hungry, the bulbul looked at the cuckoo and mechanically grumbled, "Stay away from the fruit, it is mine." Then, he went back to inspecting the crimson bulbs while muttering his flower song.

"First comes the bud, then the flower, and then the fruit, which I will devour."

The cuckoo looked at him in disgust. There was no reasoning with the foolish bird. So she flew back home and didn't tell the bulbul that he was being silly. For, you see, his precious home was a cotton tree, which would never bear any edible fruit.

Then one day, the crimson flowers turned into a pod. The bulbul flew around in a frenzy, jumping from pod to pod, yelling, "The fruit must be almost ready." With renewed vigour, he sang his song:

"First comes the bud, then the flower, and then the fruit, which I will devour!"

By now, all the birds had gathered around the cuckoo's nest to see what the bulbul would do. These birds had been shooed away by the bulbul in the hottest of months, and they were all quite sick of him. The bulbul did not care. This was the moment he had been waiting for. He pecked and pecked at the pods, but nothing happened.

Poof! Poof! Poof! The pods burst and balls of white cotton scattered through the tree. Some fell on the ground and the wind carried the rest away.

The bulbul looked left and right, then up and down. "Where's the fruit? It was supposed to be here," he exclaimed. A little cotton flew into his beak and he sneezed. It was dry and woolly. "Achoo!" he sneezed again.

The birds on the other tree couldn't keep a straight face any longer. They burst into laughter as the bulbul continued to search for his beloved fruit. After a long time, longer than the foolish bulbul would now care to admit, he realized there was no fruit. And from that day on, no bulbul ever nests in a cotton tree.

The Water Demon

A tale from the Nilamatapuranam

Nestled amidst snow-capped mountains so high they almost scraped the sky was a lake as endless as the ocean. Its tranquil blue waters sparkled like diamonds in the sun. It was said that there was no place like the Satisaras, as the lake was called, across all the realms. Even the gods would descend from the heavens to sit by its banks.

One morning, a sharp wail cut through the silence. Insistent and demanding, the sound made its way to the still depths of the lake, where Nila, the king of the nagas, sat, deep in meditation. He opened his eyes, puzzled at the intrusion, and wound his way to the surface to investigate. There, cradled in the waters, was a baby. He and the nagas, who lived in the lake, took the infant under their care.

They called the baby Jalodbhava, the water born. He may
not have been a naga, but they loved him as one of their own.
It was here, amidst the waters of the Satisaras that he grew up.
As he became an adult, they noticed a deep restlessness within
this child of the lake, which soon turned into an unshakeable
craving for power. For Jalodbhava was a daitya, a demigod with
an insatiable need to rule over everything and everyone.

He wanted to control the lake and the mountains that
circled it, tower over the villages and the land, and become
immortal and indestructible. Horrified, the nagas begged
Jalodbhava to give up his plans. This was his home, they told
him. But he chose to ignore them.

Instead, he left Satisaras and climbed the highest mountain
overlooking the lake. There, in the snow and ice, he prayed to
Brahma, the creator. He ignored the wind that turned his
breath to ice and his hunger and thirst. Years passed until
finally, one day, his prayers reached Brahma.

Pleased, the creator appeared before Jalodbhava. "What do you desire?" he asked.

Jalodbhava the daitya opened his eyes and said, "O Lord, I want to be all-powerful. I want strength and magic, and I want to be immortal."

The god blessed him with strength and magical powers and then said, "I can't make you immortal, for what is born must die. But, you will elude death so long as you live in the waters of the Satisaras." Then, Brahma disappeared.

For the first time in his life, Jalodbhava threw his head back and laughed. The earth shook at the sound, so loud and fierce. As the daitya descended from the mountain, he set the flowers and trees on fire. He reached the lake and as he entered its depths, the waters boiled. The nagas wept and begged him to stop, but he ignored them. They fled, their skins burning. Jalodbhava looked towards the green hills and forests. He set fire to the trees and watched as the land turned black. The valley echoed with his terrifying laughter. It had become a place of torment.

Not happy with destroying his home, he now looked beyond the lake and the hills to Darvabhisara, Gandhara, Juhundara, and Madra – the kingdoms where humans lived. He strode through those lands, setting homes and fields on fire. As men and women ran screaming, he grabbed and killed them.

Distressed at what had become of his home, Nila the naga king, sought out his father, the great sage Kashyapa. He told him of the destruction and begged for help. Together they travelled to Madra and saw the desolation, the brown hills, and the blackened trees. The sage could not believe his eyes. He realized that only Brahma could help. And so he travelled to heaven.

Brahma sat, quiet and still, as
Nila and Kashyapa narrated
their troubles. There was only
one solution: to kill Jalodbhava.

A grand army of the divine descended from heaven. Brahma on his swan, Vishnu on Garuda, the eagle, and Shiva on Nandi, the bull, were in the front. Then came the gods Ananta, Hari, and Hara. Indra heard of the impending battle and rushed to join. Accompanying him were Yama the god of death, Agni the god of fire, Varun the lord of oceans, and Vayu the wind god. The rivers Ganga and Yamuna descended too, as did the great sages and Gandharvas, the heavenly beings. As word spread, hundreds of gods gathered in the skies to witness the war that was about to begin.

Jalodbhava heard the crack of thunder across the heavens and felt the ground tremble.

He dived into the Satisaras and sat in its quiet depths, knowing that no one could hurt him as long as he was in its waters.

The gods gathered on the mountains surrounding the lake. Shiva stood on Naubandhana, the highest mountain. Vishnu sat on the southern peak, waiting, while Brahma took his place on the northern peak. The other gods gathered between them blocking every exit. There was no place to run.

They waited but Jalodbhava did not emerge from the lake. All the gods heard were his laughter.

Vishnu then instructed Ananta, "With your plough, break the Himalayas so that the waters of the Satisaras flow out into the valley."

Ananta smiled. His golden crown gleamed in the sun as he knelt and closed his eyes. Then, he started growing, becoming larger than the mountains, until he touched the sky and loomed over the earth and the heavens. He lifted the plough high and brought it down on the mountains, at a point called Varahamula. The ground shuddered. The waters from the Satisaras flowed out with a ferocious roar, the waves as tall as some of the mountains in the valley. The gods fought for balance.

As the waters of the Satisaras emptied, Jalodbhava snapped his fingers. Day turned to night. The air became heavy as darkness seemed to close in on the army. The gods shrieked, but Shiva smiled.

He opened his hands and on his palms were the sun and the moon. Light cut through the darkness and the army could breathe once again. Before Jalodbhava could try any more tricks, Vishnu changed form. He became a boar, taller than the highest mountain, with tusks so sharp they cut through rock like butter.

The boar charged, uprooting trees with his tusks and throwing them at Jalodbhava. The daitya staggered, but fought back, flinging boulders in return. This did not stop the boar. The earth shook and the terrible battle continued until, finally, Jalodbhava staggered once more. This time, he could not get up.

The boar changed back into Vishnu who called upon the Sudarshan Chakra. The gold disc with sharp edges spun on the god's index finger. Faster and faster, it rotated until it became a shining blur. Then, it flew off Vishnu's finger and cut off the daitya's head.

The nagas cheered and the divine army sang songs of victory. The hills turned green once more.

"And now," said Brahma, "let there be life."

So Kashyapa turned to the nagas and told them to invite the humans to live in the valley with them. This valley, legends say, is Kashmir.

What Made the Lightning

A Khasi folk tale

The sound from U Pyrthat's drum rumbled and echoed across the world. He was the thunder giant and had an important task, to invite people and animals to a remarkable festival in the Khasi hills. There would be sword dances, musical performances, marches, and archery and javelin competitions.

Everyone was busy preparing for it, humans and animals alike. Some spent hours rehearsing intricate dance steps while others practiced their skills with javelins or bows and arrows.

The day of the festival finally arrived. Visitors came from many lands, near and far. No one had seen such huge numbers all in one place.

The excited animals couldn't wait to get started. They had been waiting for this festival for such a long time. Each held a musical instrument or a weapon, based on what activity they were taking part in. The diligent squirrel carried the littlest drum, which he played as he marched. Then, came an intent little bird playing the flute. Next up was a porcupine with cymbals, that clanged in tune to the beat.

Everyone was having the time of their lives. They were having fun and taking jibes at each other. Some animals joked and giggled so much that day, that they couldn't ever laugh again. Like the wide-eyed mole who clapped and cheered as an owl danced and swayed. All of a sudden, the poor owl tumbled and fell. Seeing this, the mole giggled so much that his eyes became tiny, narrow slits, which remain to this day.

Then came U Kui, the elegant lynx, carrying a stunning silver sword. He had paid a great deal for it at the market. He bowed and started dancing with such grace that everybody cheered. The shiny sword reflected the sun as he leapt and twirled. The applause became louder and louder, and he became more and more confident. U Kui thought he was the best dancer in all the lands.

U Pyrthat had been watching the animals dance and display their skills with such mastery that he wanted his turn too. So, he requested U Kui to lend him his sword as all he had was the thunderous drum. He only wanted it for a little while, of course.

U Kui did not like this at all. He did not want to give his brand-new weapon to anyone. When the other animals saw that he was reluctant to share, they gathered around. "Shame. Shame on you!" they yelled. U Kui was disrespecting a guest, especially one who had gone out of his way to assemble so many for the festival.

The lynx took a deep breath and handed over his silver sword.

Excited to finally get a turn, U Pyrthat's eyes glittered. He danced and waved the sword with such force that its flashes almost blinded the audience. Everyone had to cover their eyes. Then, oblivious to his onlookers, U Pyrthat started beating the drum. It was so loud and forceful that the earth began to shake. All the animals were afraid of the tremors that they ran into the jungle to hide. A dejected U Kui stood by watching as the giant danced, waving his beautiful sword.

Then suddenly U Pyrthat jumped towards the sky, still dancing with the silver sword and beating his drum. The poor lynx stood dumbstruck as his sword disappeared into the heavens.

Legends say that even today, from time to time, U Pyrthat dances with the sword and beats his drum. People call it lightning and thunder.

U Kui still hasn't recovered from the loss of his special silver sword. He hasn't been able to leave the Khasi hills to this day. Instead, he has been busy building a mound so high it could touch the sky.

One day, he hopes to
climb the mound and take
back what U Pyrthat,
the thunder giant, had
once stolen from him.

Mister Lazybones

An oral tale from the Konkan coast

The birds living in the huge banyan tree were getting ready for the rains. They ran helter-skelter trying to collect items to protect their homes. For every year, heavy downpour would destroy their roofs.

Sparrow was doing the same. She would fly far-and-wide to collect wax, the best material to protect her house. She would work day and night to make her home safe just like all the other creatures.

Her neighbour, Crow, on the other hand, who lived on the branch below, was lazy. He would perch on the tree and watch everyone rush about as they strengthened their homes. But, he wouldn't budge from his comfortable spot. He never even got his own food and would slyly make the other birds do it for him. "Mister Lazybones," everyone would call him in hushed tones.

When she had collected enough wax, Sparrow began patching up her house. She was done in no time. In fact, all the birds and animals were ready. All except one.

Tip, Tip, Tip. The first raindrops began to fall. Tip, tip, tip, and SWOOSH! A massive gust of wind swept away Crow's roof.

In a frenzy, he flew about looking for something to fix his house. He spotted some stinky cow dung. "This should do," he thought. He patted some dung on to the roof and retreated inside, satisfied at his lack of effort.

Tip. Tip. Tip. Little droplets of rain fell. Tip, tip, tip. It rained some more. BOOM! There was a clap of thunder and the rain began drumming down the tree. The smelly dung slipped away and down came Crow's home.

That night Crow had nowhere to go, so he took shelter under the largest leaf he could find.

The next morning, Sparrow heard a knock on her door. "Who is it?" she asked loudly.

"It's me, Crow. The rain washed away my home. Please let me in," he pleaded.

Now, everyone stayed away from Crow. Whenever any bird saw him flying towards them, they changed their direction, even if it wasn't where they wanted to go. Sparrow had also been warned by her friends to not pay any attention to him.

She replied, "Hello Crow, I am putting my babies to sleep. I won't be able to let you in." Truth be told, she felt awful lying to him.

The next day, the showers were light, but Crow was drenched and dejected. He went to every home on that tree. Eagle, Parrot, Dove, Hummingbird, Finch, and Swallow – but they all pretended they weren't home.

Crow decided to return to his nest-less branch when all of a sudden it began pouring again. So, he went back to Sparrow.

Knock, knock. "Who is it?" asked Sparrow.

"It's me, Crow. Please help me. My home got washed away in the rain. Why isn't anyone letting me in?" Crow paused, and when there was no response, added, "Please, I will help you at home. I can babysit, do the dishes, cook dinner, or anything else you want."

This time the sweet-natured Sparrow's heart melted. She felt bad for homeless Crow. "I will let you in on one condition. You must help me in the house and build your home too," she said. Then, quickly added, "This is only temporary."

"Yes, yes. I promise. I will help you and also build my home," Crow said. And so Sparrow let him in.

Next day, the idle Crow wouldn't cook, babysit, clean the dishes, help fetch food, or even build his home. He just sat by the window, looked outside, and watched the raindrops. He hated doing any work. And Sparrow hated that he wouldn't do anything. She did everything – fetched her food, her babies' food, and even Crow's food!

She wanted him to leave but also felt bad for him. So that evening, she sat down with him and said quite bluntly, "You have to do your part around the house. I have too much to do and you promised to help. Otherwise, I will have to ask you to leave."

"I am so, so sorry. Please let me stay," Crow said apologetically. "This will not happen again, I promise I will help you."

The next day, Sparrow had to fly to another tree on an important errand. She told Crow, "Please watch my babies. You will have to feed them lunch. I have made khichri for the babies and rice and dal for you."

"Don't worry Sparrow, I will take good care of them," he said.

Sparrow bid her babies goodbye and told them that she'd be back soon.

The minute Sparrow left, Crow's stomach began to grumble. He gobbled up the rice and dal. Then, he saw the khichri pot and his mouth started watering. The aroma was too good to resist. He gobbled that up too. But he was still hungry. By this time, the babies had woken up and began to cry. But the clueless Crow had nothing to feed them. Besides he was starving too.

He looked at the baby sparrows and they started to look quite delicious. He smiled menacingly. "No one will know," he told himself. "I will lie and tell Sparrow that her babies were eaten by Eagle."

Then, Crow did the unthinkable. As the babies cheeped, he picked them up one by one and swallowed them whole. Finally, his tummy stopped growling. His belly became so huge that he couldn't walk. He sat with a loud thud and closed his eyes for a nap.

That evening, Sparrow returned and opened the door. She heard Crow's snores, accompanied with a very muffled "Mamma, mamma".

She frantically looked around for her babies. They weren't anywhere. But she could hear them. "Mamma, mamma, we're in a very dark room," they said.

Sparrow walked into all the rooms, but her babies were nowhere to be seen.

She heard snores and her babies calling for her, "Mamma, mamma". She followed the sounds and saw Mister Lazybones sleeping on the floor with a large belly. Her babies were in his tummy!

Sparrow had to think fast. She had to rescue her babies. "What was I thinking? How could I trust him?" she muttered. She had to be strong. "Be calm my darlings, I will get you out," she told her children.

In a short while, Crow's stomach grumbled yet again and he woke up. It was as if he had nothing to eat. He went to the kitchen and saw a visibly shaken Sparrow.

"What happened? Is everything okay?" Crow cautiously asked hoping she hadn't noticed anything.

"I had a long day. Where are my babies?" she asked.

"They have gone to play with Eagle's babies," he answered. She has no clue and she'll never know what happened, he thought and then asked, "I am a little hungry, Sparrow. Could you make something for me?"

"I can make dosas," she said and went into the kitchen. But, she wasn't going to make any dosas. She was going to save her babies today.

Sparrow heated a pan on high flame and called her house guest. "Everything is ready. Come to the dining room," she said.

Crow ran in, "I can smell the dosas, sambhar, and the coconut chutney, so delicious." For a minute, he forgot all about the babies he had just eaten.

He sat down at the table. "Where's my plate?" he asked.

The Sparrow snuck up behind Crow, the burning empty pan in hand. WHACK! She hit him on the back.

Pop! Pop! Pop! Out came her beloved babies, one by one. She hit the deceitful Crow once again and he stumbled.

"How dare you come into my home and eat my children," she roared. "HOW DARE YOU!"

She kept whacking him with the pan, even as Crow ran towards the door and out of her home. The neighbours gathered outside. Everyone was watching – Eagle, Parrot, Dove, Hummingbird, Finch, and Swallow.

Dove said: "You Crow, are always up to no good. You have spoilt the name of the other crows."

"You should be ashamed of yourself for taking advantage of someone's kindness!" yelled Parrot.

"Begone, Mister Lazybones," Eagle ordered, "Never ever show yourself here again!"

The birds squawked, flapped their wings, and pushed him out of the tree. The treacherous Crow was banished, for he had betrayed someone who had invited him into their home.

Injured and friendless, Crow limped off in search of a new home.

This time, he promised himself, he would do a better job at being a neighbour.

Yajooj and Majooj

A tale from the Quran

The kind and just king Dhul-Qarnayn's journey had taken him to the ends of the earth. First, he went towards the West, where the sun set in a muddy spring. Then, he turned his horse around to face the East, where the sun rises.

Finally, Dhul-Qarnayn, or 'one who possesses two horns', turned North towards the mountains that rose up against the horizon.

The road wound this way and that until it reached a valley between two mountains. There, lived a group of people who spoke a strange language, one the king had never heard before. They surrounded him and begged him to help. They gestured and wrung their hands, until he realized what they were trying to say.

The people were being tormented by the Yajooj and Majooj, creatures that came in odd shapes and sizes.

Some were as tall as a cedar tree and some were half the size of man, with teeth as sharp as fangs. They had strange, long ears. One ear was hairless on the outside and hairy on the inside, which they used as a mattress to sleep on. The other ear was hairy on the outside and hairless on the inside that they used as a cover. Their tails were long and sharp, as were their claws that could cut through the toughest metal.

The Yajooj and Majooj would eat anything and everything they could find – horses and livestock, wild animals, scorpions, fruits, vegetables, and crops. No, it did not seem like the Yajooj and Majooj were human, neither were they like djinn. But there were many, and it was said that only Allah knew how many there were.

The people wrung their hands and begged King Dhul-Qarnayn to build a wall between their homes and the Yajooj and Majooj. They would pay him a tribute if he agreed to do so, they said using sign language.

The king shook his head. He did not want any payment. "I want all of you to help me build the wall," he said. "Now, bring me blocks of iron." For days and nights, they built the wall, stacking the iron blocks, one over the other, in the valley between the two mountains. Until, finally, the valley was blocked. They then blew at the iron wall with their bellows until it turned red-hot. Finally, Dhul-Qarnayn poured molten lead over the wall, sealing all the gaps, so that the Yajooj and Majooj may never pass through.

The next day, the people heard scratching along the wall. It was the Yajooj and Majooj. First, the creatures tried climbing the wall, but it was so high that they kept slipping and falling. Then, they started digging with their nails, scrabbling to break through. The noise echoed across the wall. All day they scratched the wall and it became thinner and thinner until they could almost see the sun on the other side.

As dusk fell and the sun set, the Yajooj and Majooj disappeared. Their king had told them to rest, for the wall was really thin now and he was sure that they would be able to break through the next day. So, the Yajooj and Majooj slept on their ears, flicking their hairy tails, dreaming of when they would break through.

At night, Allah strengthened the wall so that the next day the Yajooj and Majooj had to start once again. They dug and dug until the wall became thin, resting only in the night. The following day, the wall had become strong once again. Day after day, the Yajooj and Majooj tried to break through. The people waited, in fear.

Then, King Dhul-Qarnayn told the people they were protected by Allah. For, every night, while the Yajooj and Majooj slept, He would strengthen the wall so that it may never break. But, he said, there will come a time when it will break. It is said that then the Yajooj and Majooj will devour the lands. They will drink all the water and kill everything in their sight. Only those that have faith and do good deeds will be saved.

Until then, the Yajooj and
Majooj will scratch at the wall
every day, till it nearly breaks,
only to find that Allah has
strengthened it once again.

Monster's Cauldron

A story from the Janamsakhis

Bhai Mardana was playing a beautiful melody on his rebab when all of a sudden his stomach began to grumble. He was walking through the rocky and rugged mountainous terrain of the Vindhyas with Bhai Bala and the holy saint Guru Nanak.

They had been on the road for sometime now, travelling from village to village across the country to spread Guru Nanak's message of peace and compassion. People waited to catch a glimpse of the great saint for he was a man who could heal anyone.

The journey had been long and arduous and, now, Mardana was hungry. All he wanted was to find some food. So, he requested Bhai Bala and Guru Nanak to wait while he went into the forest to gather some fruits. Meanwhile, Bala rested under a tree as Guru Nanak took a seat, shut his eyes, and meditated.

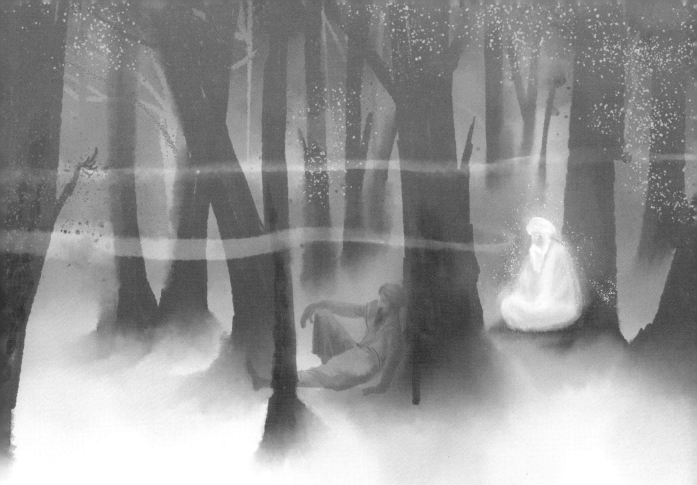

It so happened that this new strange land was terrorized by a cannibal named Kauda. The area where they stopped was in fact an abandoned village. But they did not know it then.

As Mardana made his way through the forest his stomach growled louder than before. Suddenly, the air became dense and a little tense. A numbing wind blew past and Mardana felt a chill down his spine. He realized he was lost in the wilderness. Frantic, he tried to find the right path, walking left and then right, sometimes forwards and then backwards. But, nothing looked familiar.

In a distance, he spotted a shadow. As the figure came closer, it took the form of a towering man with unkempt, matted, jet black hair. He had flaming eyes. He seemed like a man, but wasn't. It was Kauda, the cannibal.

Kauda leapt and grabbed Mardana by the neck. He struggled, tried to breathe and wriggle out of Kauda's grip, but the cannibal was far too strong. His laughter shook the earth as he bellowed: "I am going to make a meal out of you today."

He dragged Mardana like a weightless sack down a path littered with fragments of broken skulls and bones of arms, hands, legs, and feet. Mardana gulped and began to tremble.

When they reached Kauda's hut, the cannibal tied Mardana to a tree and went off to gather wood to heat the cauldron just right.

Mardana looked around. Kauda's lair was surrounded by heaps of bones. His front door had a necklace made of finger bones. A treasure chest filled with precious jewellery and gold coins lay in a corner. These must belong to all his victims, Mardana thought and gulped for air.

As Kauda chopped wood, Mardana grew scared, but he shut his eyes, took a deep breath, and began to pray.

Back at the abandoned village, Guru Nanak knew something had gone wrong. "Bala, we must go find Mardana at once. He needs us!" Bala swiftly got up and the two walked into the forest. Guru Nanak knew exactly where to go and quickly found the path littered with bones. Then, he saw a cauldron in a corner, Kauda collecting wood, and Mardana tied to a tree.

Kauda saw Bala and Guru Nanak and chuckled to himself. "This is my lucky day." For now, he had three humans to eat.

Kauda grinned, showing his sharp, pointy teeth as he lit the fire underneath a cauldron full of oil. As flames danced around the wood, the cannibal's eyes gleamed reflecting the fire.

Guru Nanak and Bala were walking towards Kauda. The oil was simmering and little boiling bubbles began to form. Bala stopped but the Guru continued walking towards Kauda. He had no fear. The cannibal looked up and saw him standing next to the cauldron. Guru Nanak smiled and dipped his finger into the boiling oil. Kauda was astonished.

WHOOSH! The fire went out. The boiling bubbles vanished. The cauldron was cold, as if it had never been lit.

Frantic, Kauda tried to light the fire again. It wouldn't burn. He reached out to touch the logs and they were damp. He was confused. Kauda the invincible who had caught many people in the past was being bested.

Guru Nanak smiled again and began singing. Meanwhile, Bala untied Mardana who took out his rebab to match the Guru's song.

Kauda became even more puzzled. He screamed, "I will cook all of you, and eat you."

But Guru Nanak was unperturbed. He took a seat by the cauldron and continued his song. The monster became still and started listening to the fearless Guru.

Not realizing, Kauda bowed his head and joined his hands. The air became lighter and he felt something change within him.

No one had ever believed in him. People had always thought he was evil, even when he was little. So, Kauda never knew any better. His soul was truly damaged.

Then, Guru Nanak stopped singing. He looked at the cannibal now on his knees, his hands folded and eyes closed, and said, "Kauda, you were blind and have lost your way."

It was true, for Kauda had no conscience. He shut his eyes and the stunned, terrified faces of all his victims flashed before him. Every robbery and every murder. Tears began to roll down his face. His burden was lessening.

"You must give up your cruel past and vow never to hurt anyone. You must be kind and help others," the Guru continued. Kauda's hands were still joined as tears continued to run from his eyes. He felt lighter and with Guru Nanak's powerful words, Kauda felt like a new man.

He became honest, kind, benevolent, and a follower of Guru Nanak's teachings. He lived the rest of his life according to the tenets of Sikhism and swore to never harm a soul.

The monster wasn't Kauda, the cannibal anymore. But Kauda, the Gursikh.

How Bhasmasura Got and Lost his Powers

A myth from Mysore

There was once an obnoxious and proud asura-king named Bhasmasura. His dream was to be invincible and immortal. He had heard rumours that if one prayed to Lord Shiva, the god of destruction would appear and grant a boon without asking any questions. He had to try it.

So, he went into a dense forest in search of a place to summon Shiva. He walked and walked until he spotted a cascading peepul tree. It was perfect. Bhasmasura sat down, crossed his legs, shut his eyes, took a deep breath, and chanted Shiva's name, hoping that the god would appear and turn his dreams into reality. Day and night he took Shiva's name and focused on his final goal. He didn't notice the rain, or hail, the cold of the snow, or even the cuckoo, which laid a nest on his shoulder.

Many years later, much after the cuckoo's eggs had hatched and her babies had flown away, Bhasmasura heard a calm, soothing voice. "My child, open your eyes. I have heard your prayers."

It was Lord Shiva, the destroyer of evil, in all his glory. Vasuki, the scaly snake, hissed as it coiled around his blue neck. The crescent moon lay nestled in his crown, and he held a trident in his hand. "What boon can I grant you as a reward for your devotion?" he asked.

Unable to contain his excitement, Bhasmasura blurted out, "My lord, I want to be immortal."

Taken aback, Shiva said, "I am sorry. This is one wish I cannot grant. It is against the laws of nature for everyone who is born must die."

Bhasmasura thought for a minute. "Then, I want to be able to turn my enemies into ashes with a mere touch," he declared.

"As you wish," Shiva said with a smile, pointing to Bhasmasura's right hand.

Bhasmasura was itching to test his magical power and reached out to touch the peepul tree that had given him shelter for so many years. It disappeared in a cloud of ashes. Bhasmasura laughed. "I am the most powerful being. I can destroy anyone!" He roared with joy, as Shiva looked dumbstruck.

Nothing could stop the asura-king now, as he touched whatever he could see – flowers, anthills, and bushes. Then, he looked at Shiva.

"Now, I will turn you to ashes and take your place on Mount Kailash." The shocked Shiva backed away slowly and then started to run. Bhasmasura followed, his right hand outstretched.

Shiva searched for a place to hide until he found shelter in a plantation. The god was astounded by the destruction the asura-king left as he searched for him. Everything around Bhasmasura had been reduced to ashes. Shiva asked Lord Vishnu, the protector of all the realms, for help.

Bhasmasura had nearly caught up with Shiva when he spotted a lovely woman dressed in white. She was plucking golden marigolds and red hibiscus flowers. Stunned by her beauty, Bhasmasura forgot all about Shiva.

It took him some time to string words together. "Who … who are you?"

Alarmed, Mohini exclaimed, "How dare you come to me and ask me my name. You tell me your name first. Who are you?"

"My name is Bhasmasura, I am the most powerful asura in this land," he said. "Please tell me your name."

"My name is Mohini," she said.

"Such a beautiful name, Mohini. What brings you to this garden?" asked a now-lovestruck Bhasmasura. Then, out of the blue and without waiting for a reply, he blurted, "I must marry you."

Mohini laughed, "You are too kind, my lord. Shouldn't you at least be clean before you ask for my hand in marriage? You have dirt on you."

In pursuit of Shiva all over the earth and heavens, Bhasmasura's appearance had become quite filthy. His feet were caked in mud and clothes covered in layers of dust.

The asura-king searched for a water body. But, he had turned lakes, rivers, and wells into ashes, and the rest had magically become dry. Finally, he spotted a spring. Mohini instructed him to pour three handfuls of water over his head. Bhasmasura obediently cupped his hand like a bowl and dipped it into the stream. As he raised his hands over his head he gave Mohini a toothy grin. He'd forgotten all about Shiva.

Then, he slipped and accidentally touched his head with his right hand.

The next second, there
was no Bhasmasura,
just a pile of ashes,
where he once stood.

Shiva emerged from his hideout, and Mohini transformed
into Lord Vishnu.

"Lord Vishnu! Thank you. Bhasmasura would have destroyed
me had you not come to the rescue," exclaimed Shiva.

"Anytime, my friend," Vishnu replied with a smile. "Though,
next time, think before you grant a wish." Then, he disappeared.

Shiva let out a sigh of relief and retreated to Mount Kailash.
From that day on, when it came to granting boons, he tread with
caution. For not everyone can wield magic even if they think they
are ready for it.

The Monkey, the Giant, and the Lost Traveller

An adventure from Eastern India

The monkey had been sitting on the tree for a while. His tail twitched this way and that as he cradled a pot in his arms. Every once in a while, he would dip his hand into the pot, pull out a fistful of fried peas, and shove them into his mouth.

A traveller appeared on the horizon, walking fast, almost trying to outrun the burning sun. His clothes had seen better days and his shoes were at the end of their journey too. He sat under the tree and noticed the monkey eating fried peas.

"Mister Monkey," he shouted up into the tree. "Would you share some of the peas? I haven't eaten all day." The monkey was too busy chewing so, instead of replying, jumped down, settled next to the man, and offered him the peas. The man made quick work of them. As he got up and collected his belongings, the monkey piped up: "Mister, why are you in such a hurry to run away with my peas?"

The man was puzzled. Whatever did the monkey mean? "Mister Monkey," he said. "How can I return peas that I have already eaten?"

The monkey shrugged. "Either give me my peas or carry me on your shoulders and take me wherever I want to go."

The man had no choice. So he knelt down and let the monkey climb on to his shoulders. The traveller soon realized that the monkey was very demanding. At every crossroad, he would pull the man's ears in the direction he wanted to go. Left ear to turn left, and the right ear to go right. If the man stopped to catch his breath, the monkey would whip him with his tail. "Move faster," he would command from the man's shoulders.

Sometime later, they met a musician carrying drums to sell at the market. "I want a drum," the monkey demanded. "Get me one or return my peas." The man had no choice to buy the monkey a drum.

They soon came upon a small village and saw an old woman with a winnowing fan, a basket used to separate grains. She was sorting the chaff from the wheat. The monkey pulled the man's ears and asked for the winnowing fan. "Buy it for me," he said. "Or return my peas." The man had no choice but to buy him the basket.

The sun had been making its way across the sky and was now getting ready to set. The man was getting worried, but the monkey wanted to keep going. They passed a man selling rope, so long and thick it looked like a giant python. The monkey wanted that too. "Or return my peas," he ordered. Again, the man had to give in.

Now loaded with a big drum, basket, long coil of thick rope, and a nagging monkey who kept pulling his ears, the man tried to walk as fast as possible. Night soon fell and the monkey directed him to a nearby forest.

They spotted a mansion in the distance. It was deserted, quiet, and dark. Vines made their way across the walls and a huge oak tree stood next to it. The monkey directed the man to go to the tree.

Asking the man to hold on to his tail, the monkey scampered up the tree and to the roof of the mansion. "We will spend the night here," he said.

Now the mansion had a large window and the man took a quick peek. It was a mistake. For what he saw inside terrified him.

A giant, broad as an old tree and taller than a giraffe, lay sleeping. Her snores shook the mansion to its very foundations. Her teeth were sharper than a cat's claws, all the better for eating people with. Next to her, tied to a cot and fast asleep was a lady, more beautiful than the moon that had now risen in the sky.

The monkey pulled the man's ear. He wanted water. So the man gave him his copper bottle. The monkey took a few sips and then, much to the man's horror, threw the remaining water on the giant.

She woke up with a start and looked around. "Was it raining? Well, it must have stopped," the giant muttered and went back to sleep.

The man squealed in fear. "This is it," he thought. "She is going to eat me." To make matters worse, the monkey threw the copper bottle at the giant's head. It hit her with a huge clatter. She woke up once again with a growl that shook the windows. The man fainted when he saw her fearsome face.

The giant looked up at the open window and saw the monkey's face grinning back at her. It seemed larger in the shadows, framed against the moonlight. It is a monster and it's bigger than me, she thought as she felt a whisper of fear worm its way across her back.

"I am going to eat you," the giant thundered.

"Are you sure?" the monkey replied, "I am bigger than you. See my tail." So saying he threw the rope at her. As the thick, long rope slithered down to the giant, the monkey teased, "I may just eat *you*."

Then, he threw the winnowing fan at her. "See. This is my ear."

The giant gulped. This was indeed a menacing monster and he wouldn't spare her. She took a few steps back and stopped when she heard loud drumming. It was the monkey beating the drum.

It's the monster's footsteps, she thought and screamed. The glass windows shattered. The giant didn't wait and ran out of the mansion. The monkey followed, biting and snapping at her ankles, but she was too scared to stop to see what was chasing her.

Just then the moon went behind some clouds. She tripped in the dark and fell into a well. After doing a quick victory dance, the monkey ran back to help the traveller. It turned out that the sleeping lady was a princess whose entire family had been eaten by the giant.

Kind and wise, she soon ruled the lands that were free of the giant. The traveller became her most trusted advisor. The monkey, of course, got his own mansion with an endless supply of fried peas.

And every once in
a while, the monkey
made a special trip to
the well to give the
giant a good scare.

Agni and Varuna

A myth from the Central Provinces

Indra sighed so loudly his wife Sachi looked up. Her husband, the god of all gods, shifted in his throne and massaged his forehead. He looked like he had a headache. She glanced across the celestial room and sighed as well.

Agni, the god of fire, and Varuna, the god of the sky, water, and the ocean, were at it again. They were squabbling about who was the mightiest. Their argument echoed across the throne room. Every once in a while, a silk curtain caught fire or drops of rain splattered Indra as they tried to make a point.

Indra held a meeting daily, a *sabha* that was attended by many gods and deities. It was supposed to be a place where great minds could discuss problems, accept offerings and sacrifices, and conduct important celestial business. This was not supposed to be a place for gods to compete, boast about their latest victories and achievements, or try to prove their might.

But Agni and Varuna did not care. They were too busy trying to outdo each other.

"I reign over the realm of water. I cause the rains. I watch over the rivers to make sure they are full and they flow through the fields and valleys on Earth. No life is possible without me. Thus, I AM the greatest of all," bragged Varuna.

"I am the god of fire. I have many forms. No ritual is possible without me. I provide light and warmth to all the Universe," Agni said, stamping his foot and sending a tiny flame towards Varuna.

The god of oceans sidestepped the flame and splattered Agni with drops of water, "I help Yama guard his kingdom of the dead. If the dead are not contained, they would destroy everything living."

Agni snorted, "That does not give you superiority over me. My fierce energy can destroy anything. I AM the greatest!"

Across the throne room, Sachi heard a low growl and looked at her husband. He was drenched in rain, as were all the other gods sitting near him. Indra jumped up from his throne and bellowed, "GET OUT!"

Agni and Varuna stopped fighting and looked at him. "You are banned from heaven until you make up your mind," Indra commanded. "Go to Earth and sort out your problems. Get out!"

The two gods looked surprised and muttered under their breaths, "Fine, we're going." So saying, they stomped off to Earth.

Determined to defeat Varuna, Agni waved his hand and villages and forests, dense and green, burnt. As the people screamed in terror, Varuna brought the rains and doused the flames.

Agni then walked on the river beds and the ocean floors. As everything dried, Varuna called upon the clouds and the rivers and oceans were brimming with water.

Agni tried to set fire to the forests once again, but failed as everything was wet and soggy.

This was embarrassing. Agni grew a little red in his face and unleashed his fury on Meru, the sacred mountain. As the rocks turn black, Varuna sent forth a shower of rain and vanquished the fires.

Unable to face defeat, Agni disappeared into Meru's rocky caves and was never seen again.

Legends say that is why, even today, one can see sparks when steel strikes black rock. That is just Agni trying to prove that he is still the greatest of all.

The Stubborn Strand of Hair

A folk tale from Southern India

The landlord was angry once again. He couldn't find any labourers to till his land. The canals on his property were also running dry because people refused to work for him. And now, the tenants who had leased his land were refusing to help. It wasn't their fault, really. Come to think of it, one could understand why all the labourers ran in the other direction when they spotted the landlord. For he was not the most pleasant.

He had all the land and money in the world but, was as stingy as a desert is with water.

Frustrated, the landlord paced the verandah of his house, trying to come up with a solution. Paying the tenants or labourers their due never crossed his mind. For if it had, life would have been so much simpler. At that moment, he saw a sage known for his magical powers. The landlord invited him in for a meal and asked him for help as soon as he had finished eating.

The sage thought for a moment and then said, "You must call upon a brahmarakshas. He will do the work of a 100 men and women." Then, he handed the landlord a complicated mantra. "Speak this incantation every morning and night for three months. When the brahmarakshas appears, he will have to do your bidding."

Now, brahmarakshasas are demons that should not be taken lightly. For not only are they mighty, they also possess the knowledge of the Vedas and the Puranas. They are clever and few have ever been outwitted by humans.

The landlord did not care. He grabbed the mantra and chanted it every morning and night for three months.

Then on the first night of the fourth month, a terrible storm swept through the landlord's farms. When it ended, there stood before him a hideous creature. Tall, and balding, he had shiny white teeth with sharp edges. When he spoke, the very earth trembled. The landlord gulped. This was not what he had expected.

"Why have you summoned me, kind sir?" the brahmarakshas rumbled, in as polite a tone as he could manage. Truth be told, he was quite irritated for the landlord's diligent prayers had not let him sleep in three months.

"I want you to work for me," the landlord said. "I want you to do as I say."

The brahmarakshas bowed low and then displayed his teeth in a frightening smile. "As you wish. But you must promise me one thing."

"What?" asked the landlord.

"You must always give me work to do. As soon as one job is done, you must give me the second without a moment to spare. If you do not, I will eat you."

The landlord agreed. He had enough work to keep the brahmarakshas occupied for the rest of his life.

First, the landlord commanded the brahmarakshas to plough all the fields he owned across 20 villages. That should keep him occupied for at least a few months, he thought. The brahmarakshas bowed and vanished and the landlord went in for dinner. Barely had he eaten a handful of rice and rasam that the creature reappeared.

Tap ... Tap

"I am done," he said and waited.

The landlord nearly choked. It had been just two hours. He took a deep breath. It doesn't matter, he thought. I have more work for him. He instructed the demon to dig and replant all the flowers in the gardens of all his homes across 20 villages.

"That was easy," the brahmarakshas said, reappearing so suddenly that he scared the landlord half to death. It hadn't even been an hour.

Dig all the canals in all the 20 villages, the landlord instructed. They have to be so deep that there is enough water for 100 summers. The brahmarakshas bowed and disappeared.

The landlord was worried now. He knew the brahmarakshas would finish this task too and he was running out of chores. "I will be eaten," he thought. "If only I had hired people to do the work instead." He started wailing and his wife came rushing out to see what had happened.

When the landlord told her of his predicament, she smiled and consoled him. "When you are done with all your tasks, send him to me. I will give him something that is sure to keep him occupied for a long, long time," she said. The landlord laughed and sneered at his wife, for he was mean that way. "What does she know," he thought.

Sure enough, the brahmarakshas appeared a few hours later. He had finished his chore and now wanted a new task. The landlord looked around, desperate to come up with another task when he noticed two tall palm trees and a dry, abandoned tank near his home.

"Aha!" he exclaimed and said, "Make that tank as deep as both these palm trees combined and repair the embankment." This should keep him occupied, he thought. But, once again, the creature finished that task in no time.

The brahmarakshas rubbed his hands in glee. He knew the landlord was running out of work and was looking forward to making a meal of him, for he looked plump and tasty.

Desperate the landlord said, "My wife has a small task for you. Could you complete it for her?" The brahmarakshas nodded.

The wife came out of the house and looked at the demon from head to toe with steely eyes. The brahmarakshas felt uneasy. No one had ever looked at him like that. Then, she plucked a curly strand of black hair from her scalp. "Straighten this for me. Come back when you are done," she commanded.

The demon took it and disappeared. He went to the loneliest corner of a field, climbed a peepul tree, and looked at the strand of hair. First, he tugged at each end, pulling the hair as straight as possible. He held it like that for five minutes and let it go. The strand sprung back to its original curly shape.

He frowned. Then, he rolled the hair on his thigh a few times. That should do the trick, he thought. But the stubborn strand refused to change its shape.

He blew on it,

he stomped on it,

even put it between the pages of a book.

But the hair remained curly.

Then he remembered a trick goldsmiths used to straighten metal wires, by heating them over flames. So he lit a fire and held the hair over it. The hair caught fire and as is usually the case, frizzled up. There was also an odd, nasty smell.

The brahmarakshas got nervous. Not only had he failed at the task, he had also burnt the hair. He remembered the landlord's wife and her forbidding expression. There was only one thing left to do.

The demon fled the village, never to be seen again.

That is why clumps of hair are nailed to some trees in parts of southern India. It is to remind demons of the task they failed to complete.

As far as the landlord was concerned, he learnt his lesson and became generous. He always gave the people who worked for him their due. And, he never, ever underestimated his wife again.

Churning of the Ocean

A legend from the Puranas

A secret meeting between all the gods was in progress. The atmosphere was tense and everyone was talking in whispers. The asuras, power-hungry deities of the underworld, had now conquered Earth and Heaven.

Things had been different just a few weeks ago. The mighty gods ruled Heaven and were worshipped on Earth. Then, the all-powerful and learned sage Durvasas paid Indra, the king of all gods, a visit, bringing him an exquisite gift. It was a garland made of rare flowers found only in the furthest corners of Heaven. Indra paid it no heed and flippantly placed it on his elephant's tusk. Overwhelmed by the strong floral scent, the animal threw the garland on the ground and trampled it.

Enraged to see his gift treated with such callousness, Durvasas lost his temper. He cursed Indra and the other gods: "Just like this garland, your supremacy over the universe will also be in ruins." Indra pleaded for mercy, but the sage stormed out. As he left, the gods felt their strength and magic waning. Soon, they became weak.

The asuras had always wanted to defeat the gods and, led by King Bali, chose that moment to attack. Weak, the gods fled their homes.

Desperate, Indra prayed to the three supreme deities – Brahma, the creator of the universe; Shiva, the destroyer of evil, ignorance, and death; and Vishnu, the preserver of the universe. "Please rid us of this wretched curse and help us get back our powers," Indra begged them.

But Durvasas' curse was far too strong. Neither Shiva nor Brahma could lift it. Finally, Vishnu spoke, "There's only one thing that can be done. Churn the celestial Ocean of Milk. At its bottom lies a magical nectar. Your powers will return when you drink it."

But how would they churn the ocean? They were too weak. Vishnu offered a solution. "Make peace with the asuras and ask them to help. I will take care of the rest," he said with a smile and vanished.

So, an invitation was extended to King Bali and his asuras. "If we do this together, we can share the ocean's wealth," Indra promised Bali.

The thought of immortality and insurmountable strength from the nectar convinced Bali. The war was suspended for the time being as the gods and the asuras joined forces to churn the celestial ocean.

First, they needed a powerful and sturdy churning stick for the vast ocean. The gods and asuras requested the mighty mountain Mandara, who agreed.

Mandara was placed at the centre of the ocean. But what was powerful enough to churn the mightiest of mountains? Shiva told the gods and the asuras to request Vasuki, the king of the serpents, who agreed to help. The mighty serpent wrapped himself around the mountain, his head one side and tail on the other.

The asuras did not want to hold Vasuki's tail. They felt it was humiliating and so, insisted on holding his head. The gods and asuras got into position, facing each other and pulled at the snake. Mandara moved back and forth, but it was too big and heavy. They tried their best to hold on, but, the mountain started slipping.

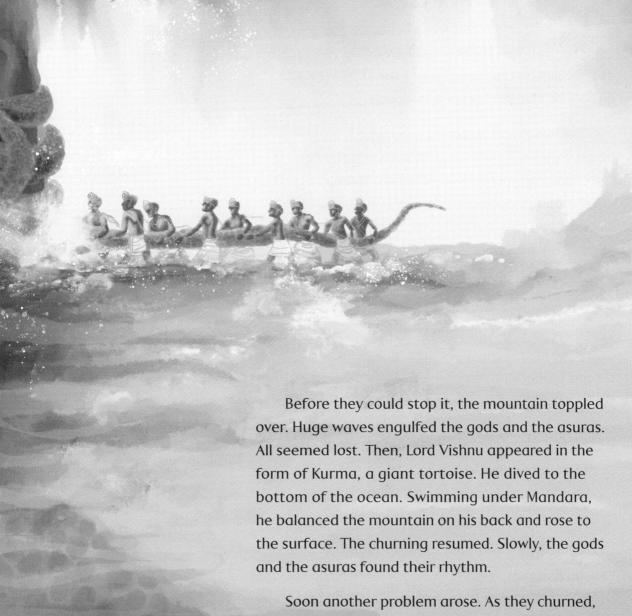

Before they could stop it, the mountain toppled over. Huge waves engulfed the gods and the asuras. All seemed lost. Then, Lord Vishnu appeared in the form of Kurma, a giant tortoise. He dived to the bottom of the ocean. Swimming under Mandara, he balanced the mountain on his back and rose to the surface. The churning resumed. Slowly, the gods and the asuras found their rhythm.

Soon another problem arose. As they churned, the asuras inhaled toxic venom from Vasuki's mouth, which ate away at their strength, weakening them. Then came fire from his breath that covered everyone in ash, slowing them down and making it hard to breathe. Seeing them struggle, Vishnu called for rain that washed away the poison.

The gods and the asuras churned the ocean and as they did, lost treasures rose from the bottom. Some gifts were magical and others deadly.

The worst was *halahala*, a poison so great it could destroy the entire universe. It rose from the froth of the ocean and merged with the atmosphere. The toxic, misty cloud of poison made everyone cough. They couldn't breathe, everything became blurry, and slowly they started stumbling and fainting. Terrified, they prayed to Shiva.

He appeared along with Parvati, the goddess of love, strength, and power. He gathered the *halahala* and started drinking it. As the poison reached Shiva's throat, his neck turned blue and he became breathless. Parvati cured him, but his neck remained blue, which is why he is sometimes called Neelkantha. Scorpions, snakes, and a few herbs and plants absorbed the rest of the poison.

As the gods and asuras churned, the ocean rippled and Surabhi, the wish-fulfilling cow, emerged from the waters. They offered her to the sages. Then came Uchchaih-sravas, a white horse, which was given to Indra. The fragrant Parijata tree emerged next, and the air sweetened with its scent. It was taken to heaven and kept for safekeeping. Then came the nymphs, or apsaras, who chose to live in Indra's court. Vishnu's renowned gem Kaustubha and his conch, also emerged, as did Lakshmi, the goddess of prosperity, who rose with a lotus in her hand.

The gods and asuras were now exhausted. At long last, the bottom of the ocean was visible and a magical medicine man appeared. His name was Dhanvantri and he held a jar of nectar in his arms. The gods dropped Vasuki and ran towards him, but the asuras got there first and snatched it from Dhanvantri.

"The asuras will take a sip and have twice the strength they had," exclaimed one of the gods. They knew that the asuras wouldn't share a single drop of nectar with them.

Suddenly, a beautiful enchantress appeared. She was dressed in white and wore a wreath of jasmine flowers around her head. It was Lord Vishnu in the avatar of Mohini, an illusion meant to fool the asuras.

She walked towards the asuras who were fighting over the jar of nectar.

"I must get it first."

"Give me a sip."

"No, not before me!"

"I caught it, so I should have the first sip."

They stopped arguing when they heard a soft, musical voice. "Everyone has worked so hard to find this holy nectar. You should all share it. Let me have the jar and I will distribute it equally," said the smiling Mohini. The asuras found themselves giving her the jar.

She instructed everyone to sit in two rows, one for the gods and one for the asuras. Then, she began distributing the nectar.

First she poured a little nectar into a bowl for a god and then walked across to pour some for an asura. But she had played a trick.

For, every time she offered the asuras some nectar, she magically turned it into water. One by one, the gods got their strength and power back, while the asuras sipped on water.

One of the asuras, Rahu, did not want to wait for his turn. He disguised himself as a god and sat between Surya and Chandra, the sun and moon gods. As Mohini handed Rahu the bowl full of nectar, they tried to warn her, but it was too late. There was only one thing to be done.

Mohini transformed into Vishnu and flung the Sudarshan Chakra at the asura. The weapon cut the asura's head off, but he did not die, for he had already swallowed the nectar.

When the asuras saw Mohini turn into Vishnu they realized that they had been betrayed. They attacked the gods, but a lot had changed. The asuras were now weak, their bodies fragile after inhaling Vasuki's poison and exhausted from churning the ocean. The gods, however, were strong once again.

The great war between the gods and asuras began to the sounds of the conch, the trumpeting of elephants, and the neighing of horses.

King Bali directed the asuras from his flying chariot, and Indra led the gods while riding Airavata, his elephant. Bali, who could create illusions, conjured up a deadly fire and its flames threatened to engulf the gods. The ocean's waves turned violent and whirlpools appeared. The army of gods froze.

Then, a soft wind blew
through the battle as
Lord Vishnu appeared
on his eagle,
the great Garuda.

As he entered the battlefield, the illusions disappeared and the gods could
see things clearly. Energized, they fought back. They defeated the asuras,
driving them from Heaven and then Earth, until they disappeared underground,
to the Underworld.

It is said that the asuras are still there, living in the Underworld, biding their
time, looking for an opportunity to take revenge. They are waiting for the day
they can pay back the gods for stealing their rightful share of the nectar.

Glossary

Apsara

A female spirit who lives in the clouds or at times in water.
They are youthful, elegant, and possess magical abilities.

Asuras

Power-hungry demigods who live underground and on earth.
Not all of them are evil, but at times they are equated with demons.

Brahmarakshas

A demonic spirit of a learned Brahmin who did bad deeds in his
lifetime. They are very clever and are known to outsmart humans.

Bellows

A device with two handles and an airbag that gives out air when it
is squeezed from both ends. It is often used to fan the flames of a fire.

Bhootas

The Tamil word for goblins.

Daitya

A clan of asuras.

Guhyakas

A class of demigods who are attendants to Kuber, the god of wealth.

Kootas

A word with no meaning in Tamil, which rhymes with bhootas.

Kuber

The god of wealth. He's also known as the treasurer of all the gods.
He represents wealth, prosperity, and glory.

Nagas
Mythical, partly divine snake beings. They prefer living close to water bodies such as lakes, rivers, and oceans.

Rebab
A medieval string instrument, which was once popular throughout Asia. The instrument resembles a lute and the sound box is made of a coconut shell.

Sakra
Known as the king of heaven. At times, he is also called the Lord of all the Gods and the Protector of Buddhism.

Sudarshan Chakra
A disc-like spinning weapon wielded by Vishnu.

Winnowing fan
A basket made of bamboo, cane, or paper, which is used to separate grains from the chaff.

Bibliography

Agni and Varuna

Agni and Varuna, *Heeramma and Venkataswami or Folktales from India*,
by MN Venkastaswami. Madras: Diocesan Press, 1923.
Retold by Priyanka Kharbanda

Churning of the Ocean

Indra Cursed, The Churning of the Ocean, *The Vishnu Purana*, by HH Wilson.
Madras: The Christian Literature Society, SPCK Press, 1895; Chapters 6–8,
The Bhagavata Purana, by Jainendra Prakash Jain. Delhi: Shri Jainendra Press, 1950.
Retold by Ayushi Thapliyal

Hare Mark on the Moon

The Hare Mark on the Moon, *Myths of the Hindus and Buddhists* by Sister Nivedita
(Margaret E Noble). London: George G Harrap and Co., 1914.
Retold by Ayushi Thapliyal

How Bhasmasura Got and Lost his Powers

Marasa Vakkaligaru, *The Indian Antiquary*, Volume II, edited by James Burgess.
Bombay: Education Society Press, 1874.
Retold by Ayushi Thapliyal

How Hanuman Nearly Ate the Sun

Kishkindha Kandam, Valmiki Ramayana, Sutra 66
Retold by Chitra Subramanyam

How to Fool a Bhoota

Mr. Mighty-of-his-Mouth, *Tales of the Sun: Or Folklore of Southern India*, collected by
Mrs Howard Kingscote and Pandit Natesa Sastri. London and Calcutta: WH Allen & Co., 1890.
Retold by Chitra Subramanyam

Journey to Heaven

The Crop of Fried Maize, *The Orient Pearls: Indian Folk-Lore*, by Shovona Devi. London:
Macmillan and Co., 1915.
Retold by Ayushi Thapliyal

Legend of the Glacier-Hearted Queen

The Legend of Gwashbrari, the Glacier-Hearted Queen, Tales of the Punjab:
Told By The People, by Flora Annie Steel. London & New York: Macmillan and Co., 1917
Retold by Ayushi Thapliyal

Mister Lazybones

A Konkani story narrated by Priyamvada Kowshik.
Retold by Ayushi Thapliyal

Monster's Cauldron

A story from the Janamsakhis narrated by Gagan Dhillon and Mohina Chadha.
Retold by Ayushi Thapliyal

The Bulbul's Song

The Bulbul and the Cotton-Tree, Indian Fairy Tales, by Maives SH Stokes. Calcutta
(Privately printed): 1879.
Retold by Ayushi Thapliyal

The Chatty Wooden Legs

The Bed, Indian Fairy Tales, by Maives SH Stokes. Calcutta (Privately printed): 1879.
Retold by Chitra Subramanyam

The Cursed King

Damodara II, Kalhana's Rajatarangini, A Chronicle of the Kings of Kasmir, by MA Stein.
Westminster: Archibald Constable and Company, 1900.
Retold by Ayushi Thapliyal

The First Darkness

Sourced from Myths of Middle India, by Verrier Elwin. London: Oxford University Press,
1949. Tribal Myths of Orissa, by Verrier Elwin. London: Oxford University Press, 1954.
Retold by Ayushi Thapliyal

The King and the Parrot

The King and the Parrot, Indian Nights' Entertainment or Folk-Tales from the Upper Indus, by
Rev Charles Swynnerton. London: Elliot Stock, 1892.
Retold by Chitra Subramanyam

The Monkey, the Giant, and the Lost Traveller

The Monkey Giant-Killer, The Orient Pearls: Indian Folk-Lore, by Shovona Devi.
London: Macmillan and Co., 1915.
Retold by Chitra Subramanyam

The Sage's Daughter

The Story of the Mouse that was Turned into a Maiden, from The Katha Sarit Sagara, Volume 2
by CH Tawney. Delhi: The Asiatic Society, 1880.
Retold by Priyanka Kharbanda

The Secret Keeper

An oral tale with many versions across the country and around the world.
Retold by Priyanka Kharbanda

The Stubborn Strand of Hair

The Brahmarakshas and the Hair, Tales of the Sun: Or Folklore of Southern India, collected by
Mrs Howard Kingscote and Pandit Natesa Sastri. London and Calcutta: WH Allen & Co., 1890.
Retold by Chitra Subramanyam

The Water Demon

The Birth of Jalodbhava, Nilamatapuranam, by Ram Lal Kanjilal and
Pandit Jagad-dhar Zadoo. Lahore: Moti Lal Banarsi Das, 1924.
Retold by Chitra Subramanyam

What Made the Lightning

What Makes the Lightning, Folk-Tales of the Khasis, by KU Rafy. London: Macmillan
and Co., 1920.
Retold by Ayushi Thapliyal

Yajooj and Majooj

The Cave, Surah 18 from the Quran
Retold by Chitra Subramanyam